MY GRANDMOTHER'S EROTIC FOLKTALES

*With Stories of Adventure and Occasional Orgies in
Her Boarding House for American Soldiers During the War,
Including Her Confrontations with the Kentucky Colonel,
the Tanzanian Devil and the King of Chacachacari*

ROBERT ANTONI

GROVE PRESS
New York

First published in Great Britain in 2000 by Faber and Faber Limited, London

Published simultaneously in Canada
Printed in the United States of America

FIRST AMERICAN EDITION

Library of Congress Cataloging-in-Publication Data

Antoni, Robert, 1958–
    My grandmother's erotic folk tales / Robert Antoni.
        p.   cm.
    "With stories of adventure and occasional orgies in her boarding house for
American soldiers during the war, including her confrontations with the
Kentucky colonel, the Tanzanian devil and the King of Chacachacari."
    ISBN 0-8021-1687-6
    1. World War, 1939–1945—Caribbean—Corpus Christi—Fiction. 2.
Reminiscing in old age—Fiction. 3. Corpus Christi (Caribbean)—Fiction. 7.
Storytelling—Fiction. 8. Aged women—Fiction. 9. Boys—Fiction. I. Title.

PS3551.N77 M9 2001
813'.54—dc21   00-066311

Grove Press
841 Broadway
New York, NY 10003

01 02 03 04   10 9 8 7 6 5 4 3 2 1

for Gabriel
from Papi,
and the great-grandmother you
never had a chance to know

Contents

MY
GRANDMOTHER'S
EROTIC
FOLKTALES

My Grandmother's Tale of the Buried Treasure and How She Defeated the King of Chacachacari and the Entire American Army with Her Venus-Flytraps

Yes, that is a story! It's a very good story that I can tell you if you want, but Johnny, don't tell nobody I told you that thing that is a very *bad* story, like you mummy and daddy. A very good bad story that is one of my best, and you know that it's a *true* story, because there you hold the brick in you hand – look, almost all the gold has rubbed off over the years – and it happened right here on this island of Corpus Christi, many many years before you were born. It happened in a place up in the north of the island, at the tip tip of the – how do you call it? – of the *peninsula* that is on the side of Venezuela, in a place called Chaguarameras. And it was in this place that I had the cocoa estate, that is to say in Spanish, *chagua*, which means 'farmingland', *rameras*, which means 'prostitutes', the Farmingland of Prostitutes that they took away from me to make the American Base during the war.

Because at that time of the war I was already a widow of several years. I was left that cocoa estate by you granddaddy there in the photograph, Bartolomeo Amadao Domingo Domingo – the one they used to call Barto – because he died when you daddy was very young, and I was still a young woman with nine boys and one girl and Yolanda's daughter too. Because when *she* died of course I had to take back Inestasia, and I took Yolanda's daughter Elvirita on top. So I tried to give away one and I got back two, but don't mind, because at that time I was a young woman, and strong, and *beautiful*, you hear? Young and beautiful just like you mummy there, with beautiful hair and skin and beautiful tot-tots that didn't used to fall down, and beautiful beautiful teeth I used to have, big and white like pearls!

So it was in this place called Chaguarameras that I had the cocoa estate, and we used to ship cocoa all over the world. Big big estate, you know? So big you could never see from this side to that, and they used to say it was bigger than a hundred acres, but nobody knew for sure. And we used to have bananas, and chickens, and goats and all kinds of things, and we used to export copra from the coconuts, but the main thing was cocoa. We used to have the little house there, and when Barto was still alive we would go for excursions on weekends, and pack up the children and drive to this estate that was only twenty-five miles away, but in those days it was two, three hours driving in a motorcar from St Maggy where we were living.

We used to like to go especially for the cocoa harvest. That was the time of festival at Chaguarameras they used to call to 'Dance the Cocoa'. You see, when the pods ripened and turned all purple and rosy, and they picked them to crack them open to take out the beans, the beans would have that white fuzz stuck up all over. So they would spread out the cocoa on the big platforms with wheels to roll them in the sun every day to dry. But before the beans could dry they had to take off that white fuzz. So everybody would pull off the shoes and roll up the pantaloons to go on top the platforms to dance, that the fuzz could stick to they feet and between they toes. But the thing about the fresh-picked cocoa beans now, was that when you stood up hard and pounded you feet it didn't make no noise a-tall, but only the soft soft little sound that you could hardly hear, like *poe poe poe*. So when the festival started everybody was drinking rum, and eating roti, and playing music and thing, and Kitchener – not the Lord Kitchener of today, but the *father*, that was a young boy then – Kitchener even made a calypso of that fête yes, with all of us jumping up first thing to sing and dance like this:

> *Hello Mister Barto,*
> *I'm coming to Chagua-ramo!*
> *It's there to dance the co-coa,*
> *and make me feet cry poe . . . poe!*
> *poe-poe pa-tee poe . . . poe!*
> *poe-poe pa-tee poe . . . poe!*

Sweet heart of Jesus! I can't hardly pick up the old feet again! What a thing eh, when you get old? I'd best sit down quick before the legs break off! Ninety-six years, you know? What a thing! But the head is still good, and the blood is not so yellow, and the wrinkles are not so bad for an oldwoman that has been a widow over *sixty* years. You see what is life? Ten children and I'm not dead yet, thank the lord. In truth, I don't know *what* Papa God will give me to kill me yes, because I've never been cut by no doctor – even though I made *eight* of them myself – and never stitched, that the one time I was chopping patatas and this little piece of the finger went on the ground like that, I just picked it up and pushed it back together and the flesh stuck, that you daddy always says would defy medical science. And I have him to take care of me and bring me here to you house, so I could have my little room with all the grands, and great-grands, and all the *great-great*-grandchildren coming to visit me and shouting down the place at all hours of the day and night!

So where I was now? Oh yes, so at that time I had this estate that they took away from me to make the American Base. But when Barto was still alive it was still the cocoa. And we used to drive to Chaguarameras almost every weekend to see about the affairs of the cocoa and things, but the main reason was

5

because that was the time when Barto had gone crazy to fight the cocks. Crazy crazy for that cock-fighting business, you hear? And we had plenty roosters, and a Venezuelan named Toy Mushu that he brought from Caracas to train the birds. Barto had the best in all Corpus Christi, and the men would come from Venezuela and Columbia and all over the place to Chaguarameras to fight they cocks against Bambolina, that was the best cock Corpus Christi had ever seen. Beautiful beautiful rooster, you hear? With bright bright eyes, and the wrinkles hanging just like this, and the headdress red red, and that was toenails, *papa-yo!* Because at that time they didn't have so much cockfighting in Corpus Christi again, except what they had in the mountains and in the bush, but Chaguarameras was too far out in the country then to worry the police. They used to say Barto bought that estate only to fight he cocks that was he passion. And something might be true in that, because that was before the time of the prostitutes – Barto liked to play the sagaboy, you know? – and in truth, we didn't used to make so much money from the copra and cocoa.

Because at that time Chaguarameras was still called *Chaguaramos*, that is to say, the Farmingland of Flowers. You see, when the cocoa made the flowers they would be covered all over with yellow and very pretty, and that was why they called it so to start. And it was just so the estate remained with the flowers and not the prostitutes for several years after Barto died. I had the overseer there that we used to call On-the-Eggs!, and he had lived there on that estate all he life. And On-the-Eggs! took care of everything, because who was I at that time but a young woman and very beautiful who knew all about cattle from living on the ranch in Venezuela from a little girl, but didn't know a fart about cocoa. So On-the-Eggs! looked after that estate, and he used to send me the little few dollars that came from the cocoa every month to St Maggy, and it was that money that

6

went to feed the children and send them to school.

So when the war started now the English brought the Americans – because at that time Corpus Christi was still belonging to them – so the English brought the Americans to look for *lands*. The Americans didn't have no interest in oil that Corpus Christi had plenty, but only looking for lands lands lands to build a Base for they soldiers. And it was the English Lawyer for the Crown that came to me – with the Yankee soldiers standing up behind him listening – and he said that I would have to give up my estate for the efforts of the war. The Lawyer for the Crown said my cocoa estate was the best place for the Americans to build they Base, because it had the deep water right beside to bring in the ships, and for the time of the war the estate would belong to them. But Johnny, the truth that I only found out *after* was how the English had *already* exchanged my land for forty-five old broken-down battleships in a kind of agreement they called a 'land-lease treaty', so the English could have all those old ships for they famous fleet. But what the Lawyer for the Crown told me was that nobody wouldn't have no money until after the war. When that time came the Americans would pay the English for the value of my estate, and then the English would turn around and pay me, but not until the war finished I wouldn't see no money a-tall. The Lawyer said that if I didn't accept this, then the only thing for me to do was to fight the Queen that was Elizabeth the Segunda one, and I said that I have never fought no Queen before in all my life, and I'm not going to start *now*.

And so it happened that the Americans took away that estate and they knocked down the cocoa and coconut trees and all the rest to make that Base for they soldiers. And then when the Americans arrived the prostitutes only came following behind. Let me tell you every whorewoman in Corpus Christi descended straight away on that place, and so too again half

7

the whores in Venezuela crossed the sea in saltfish-crates, and cigar-boxes, and whatever else they could find to get at those American soldiers fast enough, because it's true what they say that the Yankees would pay *any* amount of money because they don't have *no* sex in America, and that is why the Americans only like to fight wars.

So now you have the history of how Chaguaramos came to be called Chaguarameras,

The Farmingland of Prostitutes

Well then, the war had continued so for a good time already that I had long ago forgot all about Chaguarameras. Then one day I was making pastelles in the kitchen and I heard somebody come pounding down the door of the little house I had there on Mucurapo Road that Barto left me with. Amadao came running to the kitchen – he was only a youngboy eleven or twelve years like you then – Amadao came running to say that it was *Ali Baba* or some genie so at the door. I told Amadao that I didn't know no genie, and if it was Ali Baba in truth all he had to say was 'Open up Sesame!' or some nonsense like that, and those hinges would fall off the door in one. Amadao went and came back again saying that it wasn't Ali Baba, it was the *King of Chacachacari* that 'would wish to speak to the madame of this fine house'. I told Amadao I'd never before heard of no *Chacachacari*, and if the person at the door didn't stop playing the fool, I would mix up the boil coocoo in he panties and wrap up he cojones in a steamed banana leaf to make the next pastelle! So Amadao went and came back again to say the King of Chacachacari would wish to speak to the madame that was 'the proprietress of that farmery at Chaguarameras' – or something so – 'concerning the matter of she duly deserved fortune'. *Well!*

8

by this time I was vex too bad and ready to send Amadao to tell the King how the Yankees took Chaguarameras a long time ago – and the only cocoa that grew there now was cocoplumbs in the shape of *bambams!* – but then I decided I would go to the door and see who was this person skylarking like that.

When I reached at the door now I found this man dressed up like he was playing mas in Carnival. He had one big set of cloth wrapped up around he head like if somebody started to make a mummy and only reached by the ears. With a big ruby upon the forehead flashing, and earrings dangling, and rings rings rings, each with a jewel – diamonds and rubies and things – but not on the fingers, only on the little fatty toes! And I decided that those rings must have been made special for those dirty toes, because you've never seen such funny little things, only looking like shortie fat blood-puddings struggling to squeeze out the skins! But the strange thing now about this King was that even with all the jewels and paraphernalia he had, the only clothes he was wearing were dirty old dungarees, both the pantaloons and the shirt. And even so, the dirty old shirt – with every button gone – was tied up around he midriff with the big stomach spilling out, and a next maco ruby big as you fist like this, pushed up inside he bellyhole! It was like if these people didn't care *what* kind of clothes they put on once they feet and they belly were shining with jewels, because the King had some little baboo-boys there dressed only in what looked to me like diapers. Four of these little baboos were to carry the King around who was sitting in a kind of pirogue, or canoe, or something so, with the legs hanging down like he was making sure nobody missed the toes. With two more little baboos only to hold a palm leaf over the King's head for the sun not to shine, and five or six more behind with the big grey Samsonite suitcases that I decided must have the rest of the jewels and the dirty old dungarees and diapers.

9

By now the whole of Mucurapo had reached at my doorstep to see this King that nobody had never seen nothing like this before, not even on Jouvert morning! Then the King gave me that speech again that he gave Amadao about the 'proprietress and she duly deserved fortune', and he wanted to come inside, but I said not so a-tall was he bringing the whole of St Maggy inside my house and the pirogue and suitcases and everything so. The King said that it was only him that needed to come inside, and the one servant that he required for the King to sit on he back. *Well!* I answered the King that nobody sat on top nobody in *my* house, and he could come in if he wanted, but he had to behave heself and sit in a chair like he had manners.

So the King came inside, and when I told him that I must go and check on the pastelles I had boiling in the kitchen, he pushed a chups like if he didn't wait on nobody. But when I came back again the King was smiling ear-to-ear like if the chair ain't paining he soft bamsee no more, and now he started off to talk and talk and talk like he just ate parrot.

The King said that he had come from he country across the sea in search of the long lost treasure of Chacachacari. This treasure was forty-two bars of solid gold that the Spanish had stolen in the year 1776. So I asked the King – because I was a very smart woman, even then – that first of all, where was this Chacachacari that I had never heard nothing about it before? and what did this treasure have to do with me, a poor widow that didn't have nothing in the world? and then again this story was only smelling like toejam to me yes, because 1776 was the year the English took Corpus Christi and the rest of these islands from Spain, that they weren't worrying about nothing a-tall at that time except how to hold on to these islands that they owned.

'Ah-ha!' said this King now like if somebody was scratching he back. *'Precisely!'* So I asked the King what did he mean by all

these 'ah-has' and 'preciselies'. The King said to me that was precisely how the treasure of Chacachacari came to be buried at Chaguarameras. What the King said was that this Chacachacari island had belonged to Spain at that time too – that was the year of 1776 – that Spain was afraid to lose that island like all the rest. And that was how the Spanish ship, the one they called the *María Estrella del Mar* – and I remembered hearing about this ship from the history of Corpus Christi – that this *María* had stopped at Chacachacari on she way to defend Corpus Christi against the English, that in case they lost that Chacachacari too, at least they would still have the treasure.

So the King stopped now like if he'd already proven everything clean clean. He was sitting up straight in the chair like he wanted to jook he head through the roof, and he clapped he hands twice – *bam bam* – and just then one of the little babooboys came running with a map. 'You see, good madame,' said this King, 'you know as good as me that the Spanish ship, the *María Estrella del Mar*, was sunk by the English off the north coast of Corpus Christi, is that not correct?' And I told him that I thought so. '*Ah-ha!*' said the King again smiling. 'Here I have a map that shows precisely without any questions the place where the treasure was buried by two Spanish soldiers that escaped that *María Estrella* when she was sinking down in the sea. And this map says the treasure was bury precisely on the approximate location of that farmery of which *you* are the sole proprietress!' So the King made a big show to snap open the map like this and he stretched it out across the table, and when I looked good I saw that in truth, right there where the red X was marked, was just where was Chaguarameras!

But as soon as I could catch my breath I told the King straight away – because I didn't want *no* bub-ball – that it wasn't me he had to consult with about that treasure, it was the American soldiers who took that estate away a long time ago to build they

11

Base. So the King asked me if the Americans paid me any money for that land, and I said no, that they were waiting for the war to finish. The King went on with some more 'ah-has' now, and he said that therefore the Americans owned everything *above* the ground, but that I was still the rightful owner of everything *below*, and that was why the treasure still belonged duly to me. But I told the King I was not about to fight no American Army – not even for forty-two gold bricks! – and then again, that map was only saying that the treasure was buried *somewhere* near Chaguarameras, but it didn't tell me *where* was the place to dig. 'Well,' said this King, 'it is certainly clear to me that you are a very very intelligent woman and not foolheavy' – and I said yes, *that* is a fact – 'and therefore you will certainly see the wisdom of this proposition that I have for you.' Now the King clapped he hands again – *bam bam* – and a next little baboo-boy came running with a funny machine that looked like the vacuum cleaners they have now of days, except not so fat, and it was only blinking the lights and making funny noises.

Sweet heart of Jesus! When I saw this machine now I quick forgot *all* the questions I had for this King, because I was only watching at the lights and hearing the machine speak! The King asked me for some few coins, so I took out the little money that I used to keep between my tot-tots tied up in a kerchief, which was several of those big brown English coins that we were still using in Corpus Christi then. The King told me now to go and pitch them out the window as far as I could throw, and he would talk to he machine and find them, every one, but I said not so a-tall was I going to throw good money out the window for those people waiting outside to grab it up and run home before the King even got a chance to stand up out he chair, far less to start to talk to he machine! The King said that in truth he forgot about those people waiting outside, so for me to hide the coins all over the house, and the machine would tell him precisely where to find them. And so I did just that. Now the King started to talk to he machine, and in no time a-tall the King found out where was hidden every *one* of those coins, even the one I dropped in the chamberpot beneath my bed that still had in a little weewee from last night, that I didn't think *nobody* would think to look inside there! So when I saw this thing going on now inside my own house, I was ready to do *anything* the King told me.

What he said was for us to go first to the Americans and explain everything so there wouldn't be no bub-ball, and then we could start to look with he machine, and when we found the treasure divide it in half and take out the twenty-one bars each. But I told the King there wasn't no use for me to go quite to Chaguarameras because I had the children to take care of – and anyway I didn't speak the language of he machine so I wouldn't be no use to nobody a-tall – so for him to go and say to the Yankees that I had given him permission to look for that treasure, and when he found it he could take it out and bring it back here. The King seemed to like this plan good enough, and that was what he said he would do. So he took off one of the rings from he big toe – this was a diamond one – and he gave it to me to have 'for a gesture of good faith', as he said, and the King went and climbed back up in he pirogue and took off again down the road with the little baboo-boys toting him, and the whole of Mucurapo following behind like a band of jumbies on Old Year's Eve morning! So I stood up watching at all this commess now for a while, and when they disappeared around the corner I went back in the kitchen to finish seeing about the pastelles.

And it was almost a month that I didn't hear nothing more about the King – and I didn't think much good things about him neither – because when I took the ring to get the size changed to fit my finger, the man told me that as soon as he went to heat the metal the diamond melted like a jubjub beneath the sun! So after a time I forgot to remember the magic of that machine, and I began to think how that King ain't nothing more than a big pappyshow, and I probably wouldn't see him again if I'm lucky.

But just as I was telling myself this I looked out the window, and of course, here was he coming up the road with Mucurapo *still* following behind like they'd all walked clear to Chaguarameras and back. So the King came inside again – and he made sure he had he machine next to him blinking the lights and carrying on so – because the King knew good enough that when I started to watch at that machine I couldn't see nothing else, like a person dreaming with they eyes open that somebody has given them separina tea to drink. The King said now that the machine had told him precisely without any questions where was the place the treasure was buried, but of course, when I asked him to see the bars he told me something else.

The King said that just as he was starting to take out the treasure an angel came with big silver wings flapping all about, and the angel took away the shovel and threw him down on the ground, and he showed me the purple blow on he forehead where he got the knock. This angel told the King that he would never be able to take out that treasure until he and the widow made a sacrifice by burning ten-thousand dollars first, because you will both be multi-multi-multi-millionaires from all that gold!

But this story was smelling blanchyfoot to me yes, so now I decided to try to catch up this King in a good boldface lie. And as the saying goes, it takes one to grow one, and nobody could bake the cake better than *me*. So I asked the King how he knew it was an *angel* that knocked him down with the shovel? The

King said because of the wings. Well then, was it a man or a woman angel, I asked. The King said that it was a man angel. But when I questioned him how he knew for sure, he said of course, as you very well know my good madame, angels don't wear no drawers – and I said yes, that was generally true – and the King told me that when the angel bent over he white robe slipped open a moment, and he saw the *parts*. So I asked for him please to specify, what *parts* was he talking about? Now the King got vex with he face red like a roukou and he said, '*Parts*, the *parts*: two hairy coconuts and a big fat toe-tee hanging down between like a celestial silver sausage!' Now I told the King that was all I wanted to hear – so please to calm down and relax heself – and Johnny, now I knew not to believe *nothing* this King said, just as I'd already suspected. Because the truth, if you've ever seen an angel – and I have seen plenty in my time – the truth is that they all are *smooth*. But when I looked at that machine again blinking in the corner and talking like that, now I couldn't *help* myself from asking the King how was he to get this ten-thousand?

The King said that in Chacachacari they didn't have no money except for gold and beads and old teeth, and it was obvious none of those things burn too good – and I said yes, that was obvious enough – so then the only hope was for *you* to take out that money from the bank. So I asked the King how he knew what money I had, and he said the angel also told him that my husband, the one they used to call Barto, had left me ten-thousand dollars to send the boys to study medicine in Canada when they grew up. *Well!* right away I started to think, because nobody knew nothing a-tall about that money Barto left me with, nor what he said that I was to do with it. So I asked the King if he knew for *sure* it was a boy angel? The King said now that he come to think about it, the angel *did* flash a lightning bolt at him, so maybe he couldn't be sure what he *saw* – if

15

it was a silver sausage or a doubles with golden channa inside or anything else – but he sure did know good enough what the fuck he *heard*.

So I told the King that I must think over this sacrifice business good, and for him to come back the next day to hear about my answer. The King said certainly, that I was a very intelligent woman and must weigh up all the consequences, and did I mind if he left he machine to stand up there so in the corner because it was very valuable, and sleeping in a tent like he did somebody might come in the night to thief it.

So that afternoon I was trying my best to decide about this sacrifice, and the whole time that machine was only winking and blinking at me and distracting me, that he didn't give me *no* chance to think. I even sprinkled on him the dust that I scraped off my forehead from Ash Wednesday, that they said would make anybody drop down in a deep sleep, but that machine only went on to talk and talk and talk just like he owner. So I told Amadao and you daddy to carry the thing outside and play with him to see if maybe they could make him find some more treasure, or maybe the instrument would get so tired he would drop asleep. Because in truth the only person of *all* of us there to understand anything of the language of that machine was you own daddy – that he had only reached to five or six years then, and just beginning to talk *heself* – with the two of them conversing and discussing very serious together sometimes for three hours at a stretch. Inestasia and Elvirita – they were the oldest of the children, about sixteen and seventeen then – they came in the parlour now to ask me what about this King and the treasure? So I told them the whole story of the sacrifice and everything to see what did they think. Of course, the first thing they said was that I must consult Uncle Olly – he was the brother of Barto's father and a professor of bones and rocks, and a very brilliant oldman – and I said of course that I had already sent word to him, and he was coming from San Fernando that evening to discuss all this business, but what did *they* think?

Well Elvirita didn't say much except to wait for Uncle Olly. But Inestasia now, she'd been holding this grudge against me such a long time, and she only started off straight away about how I was a very *ignorant* woman to give away every cent Barto left me with only for some cock-and-bull story about buried treasure, and she couldn't believe she had such a foolish and chupidee woman for she own mummy! But Inestasia was only using that King for an excuse to mamaguy me, because she never could understand, even though I explained it to her time and time again.

The Story of How She Gave Away
One and Got Back Two

You see, the story goes that when I was married in January of 1913 I was only seventeen years old, and I had Nevil in November. That was before I could even reach to eighteen. And Nevil was a beautiful child, you know? With curly curly rings in the hair, and bright eyes just like Barto's own, and good arms and legs running and jumping all about the place! But when he grew to eighteen months he got sick with a thing they had in Venezuela then – because at that time we were living in Venezuela, that Inestasia and Rodolfo and Reggie were all born in Venezuela, and the rest in Corpus Christi – they had this disease in Venezuela then called *meningitis*. So Barto and me sent to Caracas for the doctor to come as soon as the child grew sick, and this doctor had not observed Nevil five minutes before he called out, '*Señor Domingo, ven acá! Los sesos estrujan a este niño.*' That is to say, 'he brains are squeezing him'. Then the doctor looked in the child's ears with he instrument and he saw the brains crawling out like a long worm from each one, and he said Nevil would be dead by next week.

So as soon as the doctor left I shaved off Nevil's hair to take out the pressure, and I pushed plasters made from cottonwool and cornstarch in he ears to try and hold in the brains, and I even pushed he head in boiling water to try to shrink them up, but nothing worked a-tall and the next night the child died. Well, I was feeling so distressed by this thing, that when Inestasia was born not long after, they had to take her away from me so I wouldn't throw her out the window. You see, I was desperate for a boy now to replace Nevil, and when I saw this girl I went crazy crazy and said that I wouldn't accept nothing to do with no child that was not a *boy*. But Papa God made me do enough penance for saying that yes, because he put eight boys on me straight away – *bam bam bam* – one after the next. That by the time I reached to *you* daddy I was crazy for a *girl* now, and I used to dress him up in little dresses and I grew out he hair in long blond curls reaching right down he back, but even that didn't help much and he almost drowned three times when I pitched him in the sea. So they had to look for somebody to take this Inestasia away, just as I was saying, because they knew good enough that I would pelt her through the window if they only gave me half a chance. So Yolanda – she was a Domingo too, and very much in the mind of the family – she said that she would take Inestasia up, so I sat down to write on a piece of paper:

I, María Rosa de la Plancha Domingo, do give to you forever this my daughter, Inestasia Rosa de los Cagones Domingo, that you, Yolanda Domingo Domingo, can have her and do with her whatever the ass you want and I will never take her away again so long as you can live.

Yolanda was just then getting ready to marry sheself to Barto's brother Stefano, so she wrote to him in Corsica to say that she could not marry now that she had to take up Inestasia, but Stefano said yes, that this had convinced him *for sure for sure* even though he'd never laid eyes on her in he life, and he would give up he fortunes and come to Venezuela to marry her and the child both. But the interesting thing about this story now was that Yolanda – remember I told you how she was very much in the mind of the family? well listen good – Yolanda's mummy and daddy were both Domingo cousins in the same way. Twice Domingo too. So when Elvirita was born not long after that it made her *Domingo Domingo Domingo Domingo*. Four times Domingo! What a thing, eh? You ever heard of any family business to go crazy like that? Sweet heart of Jesus!

So Yolanda died when Elvirita was thirteen years old leaving only her, and I said that nevertheless I had so many children to take care of I would take Elvirita for sure especially as she was four times Domingo, and of course I didn't have no choice but to take Inestasia back on top. But even so Inestasia developed this grudge against me, all these years, and she's probably *still* carrying it too.

So Uncle Olly arrived that evening and I related to him the story of the King and the treasure and everything so. Well Uncle Olly was a scientist of bones and rocks and a very brilliant oldman, so the first thing he said to me was 'Yes, angels *are* smooth, but it's also true that devils can disguise theyselves as seraphs and give theyselves whatever kind of parts they want. The point is not what *parts* the angel has, but whether or not he's an angel *a-tall*. Because if he's a diab then he has probably taken out that treasure already for heself *anyway*, and therefore he wants you to burn up all that money only to make you a fool.' The thing to do, Uncle Olly decided, was for him to go back to he laboratory and make up ten-thousand dollars of *fluke* money to give the King, that if he was a true angel he would know right away the difference. But I reminded Uncle Olly that the King was coming in the morning, so how would he get a chance to make up all of those ten-thousand dollars over night? He said that the only thing for him to do was go he laboratory right now and start to paint.

So Uncle Olly arrived the next morning with the ten-thousand dollars, and I said how that money would fool even St Peter. Uncle Olly said that in truth, that money would fool even *him* – but he was only putting goatmouth *loud* on heself by saying that, because as the story turned out Uncle Olly *was* fooled by he own fluke money as you will see – however, as Uncle Olly rightly said, the one person you could never fool was a true angel. The King soon arrived and I gave him the money and begged him please to take away that machine because I didn't sleep one blink last night only for watching and listening to him talking and talking in some language I *still* couldn't understand. But the King said he would prefer to leave him there with me since he already knew for sure without any questions where the exact location of the treasure was – and the only thing for him to do was to burn up this money quick quick and take it out – and since that instrument was so valuable he would appreciate leaving him there in the corner, but he would explain to him and make sure he machine understood that he must behave heself good and no more noise and winking.

But I don't know *what* the King said to that thing yes, because as soon as he left now the machine started off to wink and blink and talk at me more than he ever did before, until I thought I was soon to go vie-kee-vie! And I didn't get no more sleep for the next week that I couldn't *wait* for that King to come back and take him away. Now when he *did* arrive he was vex vex and bawling like he'd just sat down on a live coalpot, and he showed me the blow he received on the shoulder this time. The King said that the angel had increased the price now to fifteen-thousand for the sacrifice, and when I told him that ten-thousand was all I had in the world, he told me I should have thought about that before I tried to pass off fluke money on a real angel! He said that I would have to borrow the rest if I ever wanted to see them twenty-one bars. Well, I told the King that I would have to think about this for two more days, and I begged him to please take that fucking machine away but he wouldn't.

So I sent for Uncle Olly to tell him what happened, and what did he think? Uncle Olly said now that maybe this King had something for true, because nobody, not even he – *again!* – could tell that money was not real, and could he please see that treasure map? So I gave it to him and Uncle Olly studied it close and said that he would have to take that map back to he laboratory and test the ink to find out when it was drawn, and if in fact it *was* 1776 like the King said, then he was telling the truth for sure for sure, and if that was the case Uncle Olly said *he* would provide the remaining five-thousand dollars to make the angel happy. Uncle Olly also said that he would look into that machine and make some science on him to find out how it was he talked so much, and I began a novena that same night I was so happy, and I slept for the first time in almost two weeks!

Well, exactly what happened that you would expect. Uncle Olly spent the next two days and two nights watching at that machine, and he forgot *all* about the map. So when the time came Uncle Olly and me went with the King to the bank to take out the fifteen-thousand dollars, but we told him we would only hand it over when he took us to the exact place where the treasure was buried – and that he must burn it right there in front of we own eyes – and only then could he take out the treasure. The King said that was very fine, just as it should be, but he didn't ride in no motorcar, only in pirogue. So Uncle Olly asked him how long would he take to reach by Chaguarameras in pirogue, and he said depending on how much he beat the little baboos with a stick, maybe four or five days. *Well!* I got so upset when I heard about this beating business that I said to let's forget about this treasure and everything else right now, because I won't stand for none of *that*. So the King said for us to come with the money in two weeks time that by then he would surely have reached Chaguarameras, and I said fine but he must leave the stick with me.

So in two weeks Uncle Olly and me went to Chaguarameras, but we didn't find no King. And Johnny, I tell you I was ready to *cry* when I saw what the soldiers had done to that estate, and when I found On-the-Eggs! who was working for the Americans now as one of the yardboys, my heart broke for true. To think how that man was the overseer of my whole estate, and he had charge over forty or fifty workers, and over all the shipping of the cocoa and copra, and now he was nothing more than a gardener swinging the cutlass! So I told On-the-Eggs! the story of the treasure and described the King good, and he said straight away that we could find him in a place called the 'Officers' Club' with the soldiers and all the prostitutes. On-the-Eggs! took us to this place, and sure enough right there was the King now with all the whores playing up to him, and a crowd of soldiers standing around only to listen to the King talk. But when he saw me he jumped up quick quick to say that here was 'Her Royal Benefactress of the Domain of Chaguarameras, and the *cestuis que fu*' – or something so that the King said means in Latin 'half-of-an-owner', which of course I could never know nothing about since I only speak a little church-Latin – 'the *que fu* of the long lost treasure of Chacachacari!' So everybody commenced to clapping they hands now, and the King asked me first of all if I brought that money for the sacrifice, and I said yes, but he wouldn't see it not until we reached by the treasure. The King said that was very fine, just as it should be, and he told me how he had arranged for a big ceremony tonight for the digging of the treasure as it was only fitting. The Sergeant of the Army there had promised him a band of musicians to lead the procession, and a whole platoon of soldiers with guns to stand guard over the digging and to protect the treasure through the night. In the morning, the King said, we would divide the treasure and take out the twenty-one bars each.

So Uncle Olly and me left him there with the soldiers and the prostitutes, and we went with On-the-Eggs! to he house to wait for this big celebration of the digging tonight. On-the-Eggs! wanted to know all about this King, who seemed to him very very floozy, and why did we want to trust him with all that amount of money like that? Well Uncle Olly didn't even bother to waste he breath to answer. He stopped the car right there in the middle of the street, and he took On-the-Eggs! to open up the trunk and show him that machine! So when we reached to the little house – that was me and Barto's old house that I had given them to live in after the Americans took the estate and everything finished – when we reached the house and Indra saw me she started to bawl and beat she breast and said that she could *never* believe she would see me in Chaguarameras never again! I told her all about everything, and she said just like On-the-Eggs! that we must watch out good for that King, because she knew him from the Officers' Club where she worked and she didn't trust him a-tall, and we must be very careful to hand him over all that amount of money. I said one good thing was the platoon of soldiers with guns, because not only could they protect the treasure, but they would make sure that King didn't do no bub-ball neither. And straight away I took out *my* little pearlhandled pistol from between my tot-tots to show them *I* meant business too. *Well!* everybody's eyes jumped out they heads to see this thing, and of course they all begged me to relate the story.

The Story of General Monagas' Pearlhandled Pistol and the Tiger that Liked to Eat Cheese

You see, ever since I was a little girl I was raised on the cattle ranch in Venezuela in Estado Monagas, and that was twelve hours riding on a horse away from Caracas. But Johnny, let me tell you *that* was a ranch, you hear? With hundreds of acres and packed full full with cattle, that we used to make *fifty* pounds of cheese every day! The name of the ranch was Baranjas, which means to say 'all jumbled up together', because that was just how the cows were looking. So every holiday my father's uncle – he was a great man by the name of General Francisco Monagas – he would come to visit with us at the ranch. Now this General was the famous soldier because he had liberated the slaves in Venezuela, and he was twice president too, that you will find he statue there riding on the horse in the middle of the plaza in Caracas.

But the story of the pistol now. You see, one time when General Monagas came to visit a big big tiger came inside the house, and he walked *straight* through the middle of all of us sitting there conversing and telling stories, walking boldface like if he'd been in that house plenty of times before, and he knew exactly where he was going, straight through the dining room into the kitchen to eat all the cheese. So the General jumped up quick and he ran behind this tiger, because he was a soldier so of course he had the gun at he side always ready, and he shot the tiger so – *bam! bam!* – twice like that, but the tiger didn't fall down. He stood up right there watching at the General and chewing the cheese, and only after he finished eating up *all* the fifty pounds did he turn around and walk through the house again, just the way he came, out the door and back inside the jungle.

Well, everybody said how that was something for true, and straight away we all started to argue about who was the dead person who'd come back as the ghost of that tiger, and what was the message he was trying to give us, because everybody knew good enough General Monagas would *never* miss the shot, so how come that tiger didn't fall down dead? But after a few days we all forgot about this big tiger – except the one cowboy that ate some of the cheese and said he'd changed into a leopard, and we found him the next morning sleeping naked up in a tree and painted head-to-toe in black-and-yellow stripes – and it was a long time later that one of the servants was shining the silver and she found inside of my Christening cup the two bullets, but of course, nobody didn't make that connection of those two bullets and the tiger.

But the next time General Monagas came to the ranch the very same thing happened. The big tiger came inside the house to stalk the cheese, the General shot him two times, and after that they found the bullets inside my Christening cup. So the next time General Monagas and the tiger came to visit, as soon as the shots went off and the tiger went home, everybody ran quick to look inside my Christening cup, and sure enough *there* were the bullets right there at the bottom! Now General Monagas said he knew for sure for sure that this tiger was the ghost of General Geraldo Domingo – who was of course my godfather – and therefore there was only *one* way to kill him dead for good and give the oldman a little peace.

So the next time General Monagas came to visit he presented me with this pistol that he'd had made for me special. But

Johnny, you should have seen this thing! A little pistol you know, made to fit perfect inside my little hand, but the metal was all covered with silver and the handle only with mother-of-pearl! So this time when the tiger came the General took me up in he arms – because I was just a little girl of seven or eight years then – and he took me and put me to stand just there in front of the tiger. Well, the tiger turned around and he let loose two deep growls – *gerrerr! gerrerr!* – like if he was contemplating now which one he wanted to eat first, this little girl or the cheese. But soon enough he made he decision for the beautiful little girl, and as quick as that tiger could jump on top me I fired so – *bam!* – one shot straight between the eyes, and sure enough there was this big tiger lying dead as doornails right there at my feet! So we made a big fête that night and they took out the skin to make a blanket for me – and that tiger was so big he hung down to touch the ground at both sides of the bed – but when they looked inside my Christening cup this time they found it full full with blood that they said *must* belong to that tiger, and before the fête could finish General Monagas got so borracho they had to take the cup away from him not to drink it down!

Well! after that story now Indra and On-the-Eggs! and Uncle Olly begged me to tell more, so I obliged them and went on to relate the stories of how On-the-Eggs! got he name, and Toy Mushu, and the story of how Amadao disappeared for five days before we found him beneath the bed eating ants, and how Reggie got erysipelas and he legs swelled up big and fat like two balloons, and Dr Salizar cured him with seven frogs that he passed up and down the child's legs until they turned red red red. And then he hung those frogs out on the clothesline to let them dry so each of us could keep one for a remembrance of this story – and Johnny, I still have mine hidden at the bottom of my bureau over there because I don't like to see no frogs! – and all the old stories they begged me to give them that in the end we got so distracted, we almost forgot about the treasure.

So when we returned to the King now he and the soldiers were good and borracho, with *one* set of commess going on. The King had taken off all those dirty dungarees, and he was dressed up now in what he called the 'ceremonial gown'. But this gown was only a dirty old sheet that he'd wrapped heself in to match he headdress, and Johnny, let me tell you this King was *really* looking like a chuff-chuff now! So the drunken soldiers commenced to beating drums and blowing bugles every which way, and marching all about the place in a big confusion, and every five seconds somebody would bawl 'fire! fire!' and

boodoom!

all the guns would explode – because you know how the Yankees love to shoot guns! – and the King was leading this procession now from he pirogue, and trying he best not to tumble out on the ground. At last we reached to the place where the King said the treasure was, and he asked Uncle Olly for the 'sacrificial funds' – and after he bowed he head a few times and danced around the place a little bit like some kind of obeah-man, talking one set of nonsense about the gods of Chacachacari and such – he doused the money with pitchoil and touched he cigar to it, and that was that! Now the platoon of soldiers commenced to digging, and sure enough in no time a-tall *out* came the box. And sure enough when the King threw open the lid, there was the gold bars shining! Pure gold like gold, you know? *Shining!*

But then I saw something to take me back in one. Just there on top the pile of bricks was a single brown leaf. Right away I looked up to see if there was any tree to drop that leaf, and sure enough right overhead was a big ficus tree. But when I looked at the leaf in the box good I realized that it was a round *seagrape* leaf, not a narrow ficus one, and there was no seagrape tree in sight. So now I began to think!

And as fate would have it – or fortune, whichever one you choose to believe – Indra had given to me to eat that *same* afternoon some of the green jelly that you find in the bones of meat. She had been saving up this thing for a long time from the Officers' Club where she worked as a cook in the kitchen, because people said this jelly was very good for the *lungs*. But the thing about this jelly – and here is where the part about good fortune comes in – the good thing about this green jelly is that when you eat some it makes you push one set of farts, and stink stink stink!

Just like yesterday when Joe – the little Haitian boy you daddy has helping him in the garden – when Joe came running inside here bawling, 'I find it, Granny! I find it!' So I asked what he found, and he told me, 'The next rat.' *Well!* I had to laugh at this thing yes, because here am I in my room only *suffocating* for three days now with this smell, and thinking it was *me* stinking so – that maybe my liver or some other organ died inside before the rest of me, and the smell was coming out through the pores of my skin – and running in the shower every five minutes to try and scrub out the stink, but all this time it was only another dead rat beneath the house. Sweet heart of Jesus!

Anyway, I was telling you about this green jelly that comes from the bones of meat. You see, in those old days people had plenty manners, and if a lady pushed a fart courtesy obliged everybody to turn around quick quick and look the other way so as not to make the lady feel ashamed. So now I realized that all I had to do was wait for the next *good* one to come, and when everybody turned around, to quick pick up one of the gold bricks, quick lift up the dress, and quick shove the brick between my legs like nothing had even happened. And that was just what I did! And I walked with it between the legs just so, all the way back to the Officers' Club where they carried the treasure. Of course, it was a little bit difficult walking and holding up this brick between my legs at the same time – and every now and then it would scrape a little bit against my pussy, and I had to pretend I was scratching my bamsee to fix it in a good place – but you see, in those days we used to wear plenty big skirts for me to disguise myself, and nobody wouldn't think nothing except maybe I was walking a little funny because I didn't wipe proper the last time, and I was suffering from a little bit of bitty-bambam.

So when we reached back to the Officers' Club now I told Uncle Olly about the leaf, and I took out the brick from beneath my dress. I said for him to go with that brick back to he laboratory straight away to test it to find out if it was gold or what. On-the-Eggs! said how he would watch over the treasure, and for me to go and wait for Uncle Olly with Indra back at the house, because the King and those soldiers and prostitutes would soon start off with one set of bacchanal just now as was they custom, and that was *no* place for a gentlelady like me!

Well I hadn't been with Indra long when On-the-Eggs! came running to say the King was borracho now for true, and like he'd gone crazy. He said the King was only boasting about how in Chacachacari they had more gold than they knew what to do with it, and he was so tired of looking at gold gold gold all the time it made him feel sick, and therefore he would sell a pure gold bar to anybody that gave him a thousand dollars cash-money. On-the-Eggs! said how he'd gone vie-kee-vie now for true, and we had better do something quick before he sold all the bars. So I gave On-the-Eggs! General Monagas' pistol and told him to get back to the Officers' Club fast as he

29

could go, and don't worry about what was going on *inside*, only to stand by the door and make sure none of the soldiers and in particular the King didn't *leave*, until I could think out a plan. On-the-Eggs! said that wouldn't be no problem, because with all the money and gold flying about the place all those girls have gone wild, with every one latched onto a soldier and she ain't going to let him go before *she* could get she hands on some of that cash flying too.

So Indra and me started to discuss this thing now to try to decide what we would do. I said that it was no use to wait for Uncle Olly to come back from he laboratory because by then all the bars would be gone, in case that leaf *did* drop from some sea-grape right behind me that I couldn't see the tree in the dark. Indra said yes, and that leaf could have blown from some distant tree, but anyway how were we to get back all of these gold bars?

Johnny, just then the idea struck me! So I asked Indra, because she had lived in that part of Corpus Christi all she life, if she'd ever heard of a plant that grew by the sea only in Chaguarameras, which we used to call in Spanish 'trampa mosca de Venus'. She said yes, she had, so I asked her why did she think they called it that, and she said of course about the mosquitos. I said yes, but why *venus?* Indra answered me because that was the star that lived between Mercury and the Earth, but I said not so a-tall!

You see, Venus was how they called one of those goddesses that belonged to the Greeks – the goddess of desire for sex – and that was why the *real* name for pussy was 'la montaña de Venus'. But Indra wanted to know why as always I had to mix up one story with the next to confuse everybody's head, because what the fuck did all this business about pussies have to do with eating flies? I told Indra to hold down she horses. You see, the old time legend went that the blood of this plant had magic sexual powers, and if a woman tasted even one *drop*,

30

when the man went inside she pussy would clamp shut straight away – *bam!* – and he would never get out again, not until the sun rose the following morning. That is to say, not until the sun came *up*, could he go *down!* Indra told me she liked that idea good enough, but she didn't put no stock in old-wife's tales, and if I really believed that plant could help any pussy to hold on so wonderful? I asked Indra why did she think Barto's heart gave out so young?

So Indra and me ran to the seaside and collected up plenty of those plants, and we squeezed out the blood on all the food and cerveza, and even the channa and the plantain chips, and in no time a-tall we had the King and that entire American Army *immobilized!* Now me and Indra climbed the stairs to go in every one of those rooms and collect back all the bricks. But when we reached to the King's room now he didn't have no bricks left – but right there was all the money – so I counted it up good to make sure it was forty-one-thousand taking out the one brick that Uncle Olly had. But Johnny, by this time I was *so* vex and exasperated with this King I was spitting fire! Now I went back down to the kitchen to pick out two of the *biggest* flowers, and I begged the whorelady permission to open up she legs a moment, and I put a flower to bite down hard on each one of those King's cojones the *whole* night long!

So On-the-Eggs! and Indra and me picked up all the bricks and the money and we carried them home to wait for Uncle Olly, and soon enough he arrived to say we might as well pitch all those bricks in the sea. He said that they were only bathed in a thin thin blanket of gold that even if we scraped off all the forty-two, we might not even be able to make an earrings. Uncle Olly said that inside the bricks was only solid brass-metal, and that didn't have no value a-tall.

So what to do? Not a thing! Just drop down dead asleep for a good few hours until sunrise, because in truth we were all exhausted. Next morning we returned to the Base to give back that forty-one-thousand to the soldiers that the King had robbed them of – because of course we couldn't keep that money that didn't belong to us – and we made sure they paid the girls after they long night of labour too. So Uncle Olly and me bid good-bye to Indra and On-the-Eggs!, and we said that we have really had a good adventure there, even though we lost all that amount of money, and Uncle Olly and me climbed back in the car to drive back home again to St Maggy.

But this story was not yet finished as you might believe. You see, Uncle Olly and me were still very tired, and not even paying much attention to the driving, when we saw a woman walking at the side of the road that looked like if she was suffering from a *good* case of bitty-bambam. Because every step she took she waffled from side to side swinging out the fat legs – that I decided if was *not* the bitties, then maybe she big thighs had rubbed up too much together to give her chafe – which is very painful and no joke because I know of a woman in Pastiche who died from that very thing! So I was thinking to tell Uncle Olly to stop for this poor woman as I felt so bad, but then again if she *did* have the bitties – or if she was too proud to use the bush and she was toting a load – then we didn't want her in the back seat *a-tall*. So I didn't say nothing to Uncle Olly, but when we reached by this woman we discovered, just as you have already suspected, that *she* was a *he*, and he was still dressed in the ceremonial gown. He'd given up the pirogue and the baboos to hold the palm leaf over he head, but sure enough he was the same old King! So I was perplexed now – and thinking maybe those flowers *did* bite off he cojones in truth – because why else would he be walking so peculiar like that? Then all in a sudden it dawned upon me what that cere-

32

monial gown was all about, and why this King was walking so funny just like me. You see, in the middle of all that confusion last night to take out the treasure, the King had switched the good money for Uncle Olly's fluke money, and he hid it quick beneath the dress. It was Uncle Olly's *fluke* money then that the King had burned up for that sacrifice!

So I shouted out quick for Uncle Olly to stop the car, and in no time a-tall I had General Monagas' pearlhandled pistol shoved up against the King's cojones! I told him if he didn't hand it over straight away, I would blow them so fucking far apart that one would land by St James and the next by Sangre Grande. *Well!* I have never met a man yet – not even a little fatty King – that didn't value he cojones above everything else in the world. And of course as soon as he reached between he legs to hand it over he could walk or skip or dance or whatever he wanted, but what he did instead was to grab onto those cojones like if they were gold, and he ran for the bush as fast as he little fatty feet could carry him!

Well then, now at last we have reached we happy ending. You see, the prostitutes finished happy because they discovered the secret of that plant, and it has made Chaguarameras the most *popular* place in the whole of Corpus Christi to this very day. Indra and On-the-Eggs! ended up happy because the Sergeant was so pleased to get back he thousand dollars, that he finally permitted On-the-Eggs! to join the American Army. And if you look up in you history book you will see how On-the-Eggs! became a famous American soldier, many times decorated, and that says something good for the Yankees! Of course, Uncle Olly got back he five-thousand dollars, but he also got he machine to which he dedicated the science of the rest of he life. And even though he never did decipher the language, he machine brought him very much happiness in the end. And as you know youself, Uncle Reggie, and Rodolfo, and Barnabas

33

and Uncle Simón have all reached Canada. And just when I was about to run out of money that old Lawyer for the Crown appeared with twenty-eight more thousand dollars for Chaguarameras, and so it happened that Uncle José, and Uncle Paco, and you daddy reached Canada too. And they are all eight of them very famous doctors today – even Uncle Amadao, who is the famous doctor of chickens with that big chicken-hospital in Arima – so I think that even *Barto* got he wish.

As for me now, I have my story. You see Johnny, what I didn't know then, but I know now, is that I was born to have children instead of money. Papa God gave me money, and he took it away just as quick, but he always makes sure I have plenty of children around me to hear my stories. And that is the other thing Papa God gave me, that maybe you have a little bit of it youself? This love for telling stories. Because Johnny, it is something to give you pleasure and good company all you life, and it can bring you very much happiness in the end.

2

The Tale of How Crab-o Lost His Head

for Judy Sanchez

Papa-yo! So you want to hear this nasty story? In truth, it is a story you own daddy used to beg me to tell him all the time when *he* was a youngboy too. You daddy, and he wicked brothers, and all they badjohn-boyfriends just the same. The whole gang of them sitting around me in the big circle – still wearing they schoolboy-shortpants and they scruffy-up washykongs – all with the big smiles on they faces and they bony knees crossed before them like if I was born yesterday, and I haven't raised up nine of them myself, and they think they can hide anything from *me*. Because of course, the young-boys can't hardly contemplate nothing more than they *own* little crab-o poking out between they legs, that they can't keep they hands out they pockets five minutes together without squeezing, and stretching, and playing with it – particular when I start to give them *this* story – and in truth, that is a nastiness they never *do* grow out of no matter how long they live, *papa-yo!*

Well then, it happened in the old, old-time time, this story, and it happened in a village up on the north coast of this same island of Corpus Christi. It is a little village that you know good enough youself, because you have passed through many times going on excursions with the scoutboys, just there beyond the rickety bamboo bridge, on that same trace following the coast beneath the foots of the mountains. The village is settled there on the banks of a river the Spanish explorers named *Madamas* when they drew out the first maps, even though the Caribs had long called she *Yarra* in they own tongue – that is to say, 'the river of women's tears' – winding she way down from the forests of rain, and golden parrots, and green monkeys in the mountains, to empty sheself below in the blue Caribbean Sea. The village, as you have already discerned, is called *Blanchisseuse*. It means, in the local French patois, 'washerwoman', because that was the name the people gave to this woman living on top the mountain up above the village. Of course, they all knew that wasn't she *real* name in truth. Because to this day nobody never found the courage to approach the woman sheself and ask her she name. It was the only name they knew her by, and so many long years that after a time the little village and the people theyselves came to be called by the same name too, that is to say, the village of Blanchisseuse.

She wasn't an oldwoman. Still, even the oldest oldmen in the village could never remember a time when she didn't live in the big estate house, perched high on top the mountain looking down over the village. Just how she came to own the house and all the many lands of the big estate nobody knew for sure. Some used to say how that estate was purchased by a wealthy Portugee planter from the King of Spain, because that was long before the English pirates arrived with they long blue beards, and they ships shooting off all the cannons. And so it happened that many years later – after Spain and England *both* began to lose interest in all these islands sinking down in the sea – when the price of sugar and cocoabeans fell, and the tradings away in Europe were already finished, that they said this Portugee planter abandoned he estate and picked up heself to go back home. Some used to say the woman was the mistress of this rich Portugee – she was very very beautiful in truth – and that is why he left the estate to her. They said she was waiting there in the big house for him to return to her from across the sea. But most people said she wasn't the mistress of this Portugee planter a-tall. She was he own outside child by a Yoruba slavewoman, and that is where she got the colour of she skin, deep and rich like burned saffron. Most said the Portugee planter did not *abandon* he estate, but that one day the woman decided to take it for sheself. They said that on the same morning of she thirteenth birthday – the very same morning the woman saw she first menses – she murdered both she Portugee father and she Yoruba mother with two clean swipes of she cutlass across they throats.

She was a very tall woman. Some said as much as seven feet, but it was difficult to tell, because she always wore she hair piled in the tall jackspaniard-nest up on top she head. She was very particular about she clothes, always dressed head-to-foot only in white. White kerchief tied up around she beehive-nest of hair, white lace shawl draped over she shoulders. With she long white dress dragging behind in the Martinique style – layers upon layers of white frills rippling down she long neck, down over she ripe tot-tots, and down around she smooth, shapely bamsee – rippling from beneath she chin all the way down to she toes. On she feet she always wore white alpagats. And beneath the dress one confusion of starched white undergarments – camisoles, and corsets, and garters and such – and so many starched crinoline petticoats, they said she dress would have stood up in the corner without her inside. *So* many starched white petticoats that on still mornings you could hear the soft rustlings of she footsteps all the way down below in the village, rustling louder and louder until at last the *swoosh!* sucking the air behind her like a tall seawave, one by one as she walked past each of the little boardhouses of the village. Nobody never saw her dressed in no other way, and nobody never saw her without she cutlass neither. She used to wear it tucked beneath the hair, shoved front to back at the base of the tall jackspaniard-nest, with the handle of purpleheart wood protruding out in front above she forehead, and the long silver blade poking out behind.

Early every morning she would descend from the house above the village, the big bundle of laundry tied up in a white sheet toting on top she head. Back and forth and back and forth along the trace cut out from side of the mountain, sometimes passing for a second behind a huge immortelle tree covered in blossoms of bright orange, or a tall poui bursting out only in pink. Sometimes disappearing for a moment inside a cotton-wool cloud that had drifted in off the sea to lie lazy against the flanks of the mountain – then all in a sudden appearing from out the cloud with a *woosh!* on the other side – back and forth and back and forth until, after long last, she arrived at the banks of the river down below.

And the first thing she would do there was take off all she clothes. She would put down the big bundle of she laundry balanced on top she head, the thatched picnic basket hanging from the bend of she arm, packed full with fruits that she would eat for she lunch. Now, very slow and careful, garment by garment by garment, she would strip sheself down to nothing but the skin of she birth. First the white bodice, one by one unfastening the bright mother-of-pearl buttons following along she spine, before she would unclasp the long frilly skirt. Next, one by one, she would pull the thin lace camisoles up over she ripe tot-tots – the breeze could blow fresh and cool cool up at the top of that mountain, you know? – up over she beehive nest of hair. Then, after long last – the moment they had all been waiting patient to arrive – she would twist she slender arms behind she back, and she would unclasp the delicate lace brazier. Sweet heart of Jesus! One by one, very slow and careful, she would expose to the morning air giggling before them, the perfection of she burned saffron tot-tots. First she would take out the right one and then, very careful, the left. And Johnny, those tot-tots were so exquisite – so smooth, and soft, and delicate giggling before them in the bright morning sun – they all knew that after that first, dizzying moment, never in they lives would the air taste so sweet again!

Now, one by one, she would step from out the cripsy crinoline petticoats. She would unclasp the corsets, the garters, untie the white ribbons of she alpagats bowtied around she ankles. Now she would roll the fine silk stockings down along she smooth slender thighs. Very slow and careful, every twist, every stretch, until after long last – with one last suffocating gasp of air – she would slip down she long legs the whisper of she little lace panties. *Everything!* Every last ruffling, and lace, and silky white garment, leaving nothing a-tall but the cutlass tucked beneath she hair. Until at last she stood before them naked naked. Dressed in nothing but the splendour of she burned saffron skin.

Because of course, just as you have already surmised, every manjack and womanjill too had gathered there by the river secret to watch her. All hiding behind the bushes and the boulderstones, all hanging like monkeys peering from out the tops of all the trees – all there assembled like a band of bobolees with they eyes opened wide wide and they long red tongues dripping down – only to watch at this woman undressing sheself. And Johnny, by the time she reached to the last crinoline petticoat, by the time she finished with the last white gasp of she little lace panties, by then she had them all *bazodee*. Every oldman and oldwoman, every google-eye little schoolboy and schoolgirl just the same. In truth, the spectacle of watching this woman strip sheself down was so strenuous – so exciting, and exhausting, and so *painful* – many of those villagers realized they would never satisfy that itch prickling beneath they skins never again. The vision of so much excruciating beauty had ruined they lives forever, and after that first debilitating experience, they vowed never again to return to the banks of that river.

But just as you would suppose too, the majority of those wadjanks went running crab-o-in-hand every morning of life. They just couldn't hold theyselves back. Just couldn't keep away. And no matter *how* many times they swore that the next morning they were *not* going back to that river – only putting goatmouth loud on theyselves each time they said it like poor Hax the butcher – of course, as soon as the next morning arrived, it was always just the same. Because next morning, first thing, soon as they jumped out the bed – before they crab-os could even go down a little bit to give them a chance to make they first wee-wee – they were all already hurrying behind it. Following it like the divining rod poking out trembling before them, *straight* for the banks of that river. All dodging behind a rockcliff or a treetrunk, ducking beneath the banyans of a mangrove bush – and again, just as you have already discerned – no sooner could this woman arrive to begin taking off all she clothes, when they had already started up doing on theyselves every *thinkable* kind of nastiness behind them bushes.

Because the truth, if you want to know about all these wadjanks strutting around the place each one like the cock-of-the-walk heself, the truth is that not a one of these men had ever even found the courage to approach her. Most of them were too weak in they knees anyway – by the time this woman was ready to take she bath – to manage nothing more than scrub up theyselves to the final fistful of froth. But Johnny, the main reason wasn't they lack of intentions, trembling up the lengths of they stiff limbs. It wasn't they lack of enthusiasm, ready to burst at the tips of they busy fingers. Not so a-tall! They main reason was *fear*. They all believed this Blanchisseuse was an obeahwoman – or worse still a sukuyant, a lagahoo, or a diabless – and no man in he right head would tangle heself up with none of that. They all knew good enough that the smoothness of she ripe bamsee – the intoxication of each little nip of she jiggling, burnished gold tot-tots – was only the inkling as to what she evil powers could do. But even more than *any* of that, the thing those wadjanks feared most of all, was nothing more than the cutlass tucked beneath she jackspaniard-nest of hair.

The Story of Hax the Butcher

From the time each of them was a little boy, they mummies had warned them all with the story of Hax the butcher. Poor Hax, who got heself in that terrible practice of hurrying back from the river to he shop every morning, only to relieve heself on a defenceless bettygoat, or a soft woolly sheep, or the unsuspecting she-calf tethered quiet in the corner. And of course, as soon as he could manage to satisfy heself – in the great frustration mounting beneath he leather apron since early morning – he would grab for the big butcher knife waiting there on the counter, and he would slit the throat of the poor animal to carve her merciless up.

One morning Hax lost control of he senses, even before the woman reached to she first alpagat. He jumped out from behind he oleander bush, he face as pink as those same flowers behind he back, crab-o standing up stiff like a standpipe before him. But poor Hax never even got a chance to stumble a second step. The woman slipped she cutlass out from beneath the beehive-nest of hair, and with little more than a flick of she slender wrist, she swiped he standpipe off clean at the base!

Hax let loose a bugle-eye bawl to wake the dead. He took off running in a bolt, blood spraying out in every direction. With all he worthless companions-in-crime doing nothing more of course than jumping out bush after bush as he staggered past, only to escape the shower from poor Hax's amputation. But even before Hax could reach to the safety of he shop, he fell down face-first in the middle of the trace, dead in the pool of he own terrible misfortune. That night, beneath the torchlight of a midnight vigil, the villagers buried him there on the banks of the same river. And early some mornings, even before the first of the villagers arrive at the banks of that river, you can see him still, to this very day. Still crawling around like a newborn babe on he hands and knees – but with the same sad, oldman's sigh dragging down he face – still searching in the weeds beneath he oleander bush, two hairy huevos, and a cornstarch-plaster stuck up between he legs.

First thing, once she'd stripped down naked, the woman would bathe sheself. She would enter the tranquil water up to she knees, and using half of a calabash shell she would dip the water out to pour over she shoulders. With a block of soap she'd made from coconutoil and sandalwood fragrance, she would soap sheself down very careful, rinsing after with the calabash. Now she would move out deeper into the water until it reached to the middle of she thighs. She would slip the cutlass out from beneath the jackspaniard-nest, put it to hold between she teeth clenched tight together, and she would let loose all she nest of hair to wash it out. Sweet heart of Jesus! Johnny, every time she bent over graceful to rinse out she hair, every time she raised up those two perfect half-moons of she bamsee tall in the air – with she *pussy* of course half-exposed too, winking out from between she burned saffron cheeks at all those youngboys, all with they chickenbone-necks stretching farther and farther only in hope of catching a single *glimpse* – every morning, without fail, one or two of those youngboys would drop down *ploops!* to the ground in a dead faint.

When she'd finished rinsing she hair good and proper, she would wring it out and tie it up again in the nest on top. She would slip the cutlass back in its place beneath. Now she would climb out the river and begin all the washing. But she wouldn't dress sheself back straight away. Because those same clothes she'd just finished taking off, were just the ones she would take up to wash out first. She would soap them all down with the coconut-sandalwood soap, every garment very careful, and she would leave the soapy-up clothes to soak in a pool cut out from the rocks. Now she would untie the bundle of laundry, and she would soap down the sheets and towels and all the linens, everything a pure white just like she clothes. Now she would begin the labour of beating out all the washing against the rocks, piece by piece, raising up a petticoat or a camisole or a frilly lace bodice above she head, and she would bring it down with a hard *tha-wack* against the rocks. And since everything was pure white, it would require plenty *tha-wacking* and soaking and rinsing and *tha-wacking* against the rocks again, before it was clean enough to satisfy this woman.

By now of course most of the oldmen and youngboys had satisfied theyselves too – the women and girls had wandered off long before – and now, slow but sure, most of them had left the river to go about they business. Home to they breakfast or off to school, the men to they fishing boats or out to the canefields, or whatever else it was that they did for they livelihood. Even the local borrachos had stolen off by now, gone to the parlour to fire back they first chupitos of rum. Then again there were always a handful who *still* couldn't find the conviction of they stiff limbs to carry theyselves away. The sight of this woman beating out she clothes, the vision of she beautiful tottots – yellow-gold dangling before them like two ripe zabucapears, only the plucking of they arm's reach away – was still too tantalizing for them to turn they backs. They could only remain there crouching behind a stinging-suzie tree, or peering out from between the branches of a simple-simon bush, the pacing of they breaths and the poundings in they chests, the scrubbings up and down of they thin wrists synchronized by the rise and fall of a soapy white camisole against the rocks!

By the time she'd soaped and scrubbed and beaten out all the washing, by the time she had spread everything in the sun to dry – each garment arranged careful on the grass, spread over a bush, or hanging from the limbs of a tree – by now even the last of those youngboys and oldmen had stolen theyselves reluctant away. Now the woman would take up she picnic-basket with all the fruits, she would wade up the river, and she would climb out on the big white boulderstone shaped like the egg of an ostrich. Above the boulderstone was the leafy bois-cano to provide a cool shade, and there the woman would sit to eat she lunch: a pawpaw, or a ripe mammy-sapote fruit. A hand of sweet-plantains, or little sicreyea-bananas, or soft silk-figs. A few portugals, dillies, julie-mangoes or eden or doudou. Sugarapples, guavas, caimets, or whatever else was in season and bearing on the trees of she estate up at the top of the mountain. And after she'd finished she lunch she would lie back quiet awhile, beneath the cool shade of the bois-cano, reclining on she big ostrich egg. Then, every afternoon, after she'd finished she nap, she would sit up slow to stretch sheself awake, and she would begin to sing. Very soft and gentle, a melody sweet as those same little sicreyeas of she lunch. And every day too, soon as she would begin to sing, Crab-o would crawl out slow from he hole beneath the rock. He would sit there with he head raised up tall, because of course in those old days Crab-o – just like all the other creatures, the fish and reptiles and crustaceans and so on – Crab-o still had he head sure enough. So with a dreamy smile on he face, he would sit there on he rock to listen to the woman sing:

Yan-killi-ma
Kutti-gu-ma
Yan-killi-ma
Nag-wa-kitti

By now it was early afternoon, and all the villagers had left the banks of the river to go back home. So there was no one there but Crab-o to hear the woman sing. Even so none of the villagers could have said what was the meaning of those words of she song. Because in truth, that song was passed down to the woman from she mummy when she was only a child. Those words came from the old Yoruba tongue, and not even the oldest grandmothers of the village could remember that language scarce a-tall. Blanchisseuse didn't even understand the precise meaning of those words of she song *sheself*. In truth, it was only Crab-o, who would crawl out from he hole every afternoon without fail to watch the woman and listen, who had come at last to decipher the meaning of she words. But fortunate enough for Crab-o, the melody of the woman's song was so beautiful – so much like a sweet, restful dream – he could sit and listen again and again without tiring. Even though the meaning of the words – which only Crab-o had come to understand – the meaning, was not so beautiful a-tall:

You will kill me
My love
You will kill me
My beautiful one

So Crab-o knew, not only what the words of she song meant, but also that he must *never* come too close to this woman. Never must he come within range of she quick-slicing cutlass. Yet the melody of she song was too beautiful for Crab-o to remain hidden inside he hole. So every afternoon when the woman would carry she picnic-basket to the big egg-shaped boulderstone beneath the bois-cano, Crab-o would crawl out from he hole to watch her and listen. But only close enough that he could hear the words of she beautiful, terrible song.

By the time she waded back down the river to the place where she had left the washing it would all be dry on the one side. Now, very careful, she would turn all the garments, the sheets and towels and all the linens. And in truth there was such a quantity of laundry that by the time she could finish turning them over, the first ones would be cripsy and dry on the next side too. Now she would fold up all the washing very careful. The white linen tablecloths, the white crocheted mantles for all the side-boards, the coverlets, and blankets, and pillowcases for all the many beds of the big house. And she would tie up everything together into a huge bundle in the white sheet. Now she would dress sheself back in all the clean white garments, the camisoles, the petticoats, the long Martinique dress dragging behind with all the frills. Until at last she'd rolled up and clipped into place again in the garters she soft silk stockings, and she had bowtied again the ribbons on both she white alpagats. Now she would hoist the big bundle up on top she head, take up the empty picnic-basket hanging from the bend of she elbow, and she could begin she long, slow journey back and forth and back and forth along the path cut out in the side of the hill. Until at last, with the sun just disappearing behind the back of the mountain, the woman would reach she estate at the very top.

And so time passed. Year after year it was just the same, until one day a tragedy befell the little Hindu girl of the village. She name was Moyen. And of all the many little girls of the village, Moyen was the most pure, and innocent, and the most beautiful of all the rest. She was tall and thin with big dark eyes, and rich musala skin, with she long black hair reaching in a single thick braid all the way down below she waist. This Moyen had only reached to she thirteenth year – no older than *you* sitting there in you schoolboy-shortpants – when one fateful day she lost both she mummy and she daddy in a terrible accident. Moyen's daddy was up high in a tall coconut tree picking the nuts and throwing them down to she mummy collecting them below. All in a sudden the belt made from lianas that passed around he waist and the trunk of the tree burst, and poor Moyen's daddy fell to the hard ground below. He was dead the same instant. But Johnny, this was only the first half of this terrible tragedy. Because Moyen's mummy was so distressed now by the death of she husband, that she took away he sharp cutlass still clutching tight in the grip of he hand, and she passed the blade in a single quick slice across she throat!

So now the people of the village had to look after this little orphan-child Moyen. They gave her all the care and devotion that they could afford, even sharing with her what little food they had for theyselves and they own children. Because Johnny, this little village hidden away behind Papa God's back – despite all the beauty of those green mountains, and the river, and the blue Caribbean Sea – this Blanchisseuse wasn't no different from all the other little villages of the island. Just like all the rest the people of Blanchisseuse suffered from poverty too, and plenty hardship, struggling they best only to survive. Soon Moyen came to realize that in a village of so many hungry children, there was no room for an extra orphan-child like her. Moyen decided that she must find some way to care for sheself and provide for she own food and shelter. That is when she thought up the idea to go and speak with the woman living in she big estate up at the top of the mountain. Because of course, this woman was all alone in the huge house, and she had all those trees laden with fruits of every kind that you could ever dream, with only her to eat them. Moyen made up she mind that despite the consequences of that cutlass tucked beneath she jackspaniard-nest, she must go and speak with her, and beg the woman to teach her to do the washing. In this way Moyen could exchange she labours for a place to live, and of course, some of those fruits only waiting on the trees to eat.

But just like all the people of the village Moyen was terrified to confront this tall woman with she legendary cutlass. No one had ever dared to approach her before. Not in all the long history of the village – with only the one exception – and of course, everybody knows what happened to him! In truth, no one before had ever even mounted up the courage sufficient to mumble a quick 'bon-dia' to this woman, and no one could say what might be she response. But after only a few weeks Moyen grew so hungry, so miserable, and sad, and so distressed – that Moyen realized she didn't have no choice a-tall. And that same evening, she belly grumbling after several days with scarce anything to eat – soon as Moyen saw the woman begin to climb the trace leading up to she house, the big bundle of laundry toting as always up on top she head – Moyen went following behind her. She didn't even know if the woman was aware that she was following behind. Not until they reached to the very top of the mountain, just there at the entrance to the tall iron gates. All in a sudden the woman turned around, so quick that Moyen almost bounced her up! She stood there staring down at the child from beneath she big bundle, she hands poised on she hips and a vex look on she face, with little Moyen only cowering below in the cold dark shadow of this woman.

'Eh-eh!' she said. 'What it is you following behind me for, child?'

Moyen could only look down at the ground at she dusty feet.

She could only take in a deep breath, and mumble what it was she wanted.

The woman didn't answer for a long time. And the longer she waited, of course, the more terrified Moyen began to feel. She skinny arms and legs were trembling, when at last the woman took the bundle down from off she head. She let it drop to the ground with a loud *poof!* and a giant exhale of dust at little Moyen's feet.

'Take it up!' she said in a harsh voice. 'I going teach you to wash the clothes, and I going give you a place to sleep.'

Now the woman paused again. She slipped the bright cutlass out from beneath she jackspaniard-nest of hair, the empty picnic-basket dangling still from the bend of she other arm. Little Moyen could only take a step backwards – she was ready to turn around quick and pelt back down the hill fast as she could run – but the woman only raised she cutlass slow up in the air. She pointed it up at the top of the big mango tree above they heads, the very limbs of the tree straining and ready to break for the quantity of fat eden-mangoes dangling from each of the branches.

'You can eat all the mangoes you want from this tree,' the woman told her. 'But you can't eat the fruit from *no* other tree on this estate!' The woman paused again. 'That is,' she said, 'until you can guess my name. Every evening, when we reach to the entrance of this gate, I will give you three chances.'

A smile burst out quick quick on little Moyen's face, stretching one ear all the way to the next! Now she could dare to raise she head and look into the eyes of this woman.

'*Blanchisseuse!*' she said in a loud voice.

Now it was the woman who smiled for the first time. 'That is the name of the village,' she said. 'Is what the people call me. But it ain't *my* name!'

Moyen looked down at she feet sad again. And after a few deep breaths, she ventured a next guess.

49

'Miss April?'

'No!'

'Miss Betty-Lou?'

'No!' she said, smiling still, and she slipped the cutlass again beneath she jackspaniard-nest of hair. The woman turned around, the empty picnic-basket hanging from one elbow with she arms cocked and resting against she hips, the ruffles of she Martinique dress dragging in the dust behind, and she walked down the long entrance to the house. Leaving Moyen there to struggle and strain with all she strength, only to hoist this bundle of washing up on top she head. At first Moyen took three dangerous steps backward – almost tumbling down over the side of the cliff behind her – before she could steady sheself, and she went stumbling after the woman.

Now Moyen put away all the folded-up linens inside the tall cedar presses, she made back the big bed of this woman with the fresh-laundered sheets, the white wool blanket and a fresh white coverlet, and then all the many other beds of the big house, before she began to cover the side tables with they white crocheted mantles. And only after she'd set the diningroom table with the clean white tablecloth, positioned all the porcelains, the crystal glasses and all the silvers – each setting with a clean white serviette – after all that, the woman at last led Moyen to the back of the house to show the child she room. Only a tiny bedroom no bigger than one of the closets of the big house, without even a window to look out from, a little iron cot in the corner covered over with a prickly coconut-fibre mattress. That room had belonged to one of the slaves of the old estate, long long before in the time of great prosperity. But Moyen didn't even pause to contemplate the wretchedness of she little room. She didn't even waste time to sit on the cot a moment to rest sheself. As soon as the woman turned to leave, Moyen took off hurrying out the back door of the kitchen, hurrying around the house in the direction of that mango tree in the frontyard. Poor little Moyen was famished in truth! And of all the many fruits on the big estate – all those sour-sweet king-oranges, and portugals, all the sweet pawpaws and all the rest – *mangoes* were the fruit Moyen loved to eat the most. Even if she could have had she choice of whatever of the fruits she wanted, Moyen knew good enough that those juicy eden-mangoes were just the fruit she would have chosen. In addition, that mango tree seemed to have more fruits hanging from each of its branches than all the other trees of the estate together.

First thing Moyen grabbed up two rockstones, and she pelted them one after the next up at the tree. And Johnny, that tree was *so* laden with fruits that in two seconds she was holding in she hands two of the fattest, prettiest mangoes you have ever dreamed of in all you life! Moyen bit into one straight away, ripping off the rosy skin in a long strip between she teeth. Now she bit and bit and bit into the smooth orange flesh – not even stopping to worry about the juice dribbling down she throat, and neck, and soaking up in all she coarse crocuss-sack-dress – with she budding little tot-tots poking out beneath. On the contrary, Moyen took the greatest of pleasures in all that sweet sticky juice, bathing sheself down with it, biting and chewing and swallowing in such a great haste that she scarce even gave sheself a chance to breathe. And after she devoured all the flesh of those two mangoes, she sucked and sucked on the oval-shaped seeds until they were nothing but two hairy kneecap-bones, tucked beneath each of she puffed-up cheeks. Moyen didn't waste time to pelt no more rock-stones. Now she climbed up quick to the top of that mango tree, and she began to shake and shake with all she strength. And Johnny, little Moyen didn't pause from she shaking before the ground beneath the tree was covered over with twenty or thirty big juicy mangoes!

Moyen hurried back inside the house, she took up the small paring knife from the top drawer inside the kitchen, and she returned to the tree. After collecting up all those rosy mangoes in a neat pile like the vendors in Victoria market, all they fruits on display, Moyen sat sheself comfortable beneath the tree, leaning she back against the smooth trunk. Now little Moyen began to suck mangoes in truth! Now Moyen began, one by one, to cut off the fat mango cheeks at each side of the flat seeds. She would hold one of a cheeks like a small bowl in the palm of she hand, and she would slice a neat checkerboard pattern in the smooth, orange flesh. Now she would push up the cheek inside-out, with a star of perfect mango cubes protruding from the curl of skin. Now Moyen started to bite them off one by one – each perfect cube sweet as a cube of sugar – swallowing them down and taking the greatest of pleasures in every juicy bite. And when she finished with each pair of cheeks, Moyen sucked the oval seeds until she had sucked them dry.

After five or six of those big eden-mangoes, of course, Moyen had reached she limit. Still, she continued slicing off more cheeks. She continue criss-crossing the orange flesh, turning the rosy cheeks inside-out and biting off the cubes of flesh, until she have consumed the entire pile of mangoes. Sweet heart of Jesus! It had been so long since Moyen had eaten anything a-tall – so many days that she stomach remained empty empty – in no time a-tall that first pile of mangoes was reduced to nothing more than a heap of rosy curls of mango skins, and a little graveyard of hairy kneecap-bones. And even though Moyen was plenty satisfied by now, she climbed up in the tree again to shake down twenty or thirty more mangoes.

All in a sudden Moyen realized she wasn't feeling too good a-tall. The poor child's stomach was so full – so bloat-o with all those big lovely mangoes – that Moyen began to fear she belly might burst in truth. It was all she could manage to pull sheself up to she feet and stumble to the side of the cliff, just beyond the entrance to the tall gates. Not until she began to vomit over the side of the cliff, could the child feel any relief a-tall. And poor Moyen continued to vomit and vomit until she had emptied out she stomach of every one of those mangoes she'd just taken such a great pleasure in filling it up! Moyen felt so weak after all that vomiting she only had strength remaining to drag sheself back to she little coconut-fibre mattress – the woman didn't even give her one of the clean white sheets to cover it over – and little Moyen drifted off slowly to sleep, mumbling a curse that *never* again would she eat another mango in all she life!

Next morning, even before the sun could rise, the woman was there at she bedside shaking Moyen awake. The child was still very sick – so weak and dizzy she could scarce stand on she trembling toothpick-legs to lift she crocusssack-dress up above she head – but the woman made Moyen strip the beds of all the sheets and coverlets and blankets just the same. She made Moyen strip the diningroom table of the big white cloth and all the servicttes, the white crocheted mantles on each of the presses and sideboards, and Moyen tied up everything in the huge white bundle. The woman watched as little Moyen struggled to hoist it up on top she head – not even offering the child a hand to assist her – with Moyen following as best she could toting the bundle behind her. Back and forth and back and forth along the trace cut out in the side of the mountain, until at last they arrived at the banks of the river.

Like a little acolyte attending to the Dame Lorraine Bishop heself, little Moyen assisted the woman to strip off all she clothes. Standing on the tips of she toes to unbutton each of the shiny mother-of-pearl buttons, Moyen helped her off with the frilly Martinique dress, all the stiff crinoline petticoats one by one, the lace camisoles. She unclasped the corset, unclipped the garters, and she knelt in the grass at the feet of this woman to untie the silk ribbons of she alpagats, one slender ankle and the next. And Johnny, when at last she stood before Moyen stripped down naked, even *she* was overwhelmed by the beauty of this woman. Now Moyen sat in the cool grass to watch the woman bathe sheself. Because in truth, even though she was all sticky-up from that mango juice on she skin, she crocusssack-dress stiff and scratchy and so uncomfortable, she was too tired to bathe sheself beside the woman. Too weak from all that vomiting of the previous evening, and too exhausted after that long walk down the mountain toting all the laundry. Moyen could only rest sheself a quiet moment while she had the chance. Because in no time a-tall the woman was climbing out the river again, and now she began the lessons of how to wash the clothes.

The woman instructed Moyen how to soap-down everything with the coconut-sandalwood soap, very careful and patient, garment by garment by garment. How to soak the clothes in the pool cut from the rocks, how to rinse them out. The woman instructed Moyen how to beat all the laundry, *tha-wack tha-wack tha-wack* against the rocks, before she showed Moyen how to spread everything on the bushes to dry.

Now the woman took up she picnic-basket, she selected two ripe eden-mangoes to give Moyen, and she left her there with all the laundry to turn them over as soon as the top side was dry. By this time of course Moyen was so tired that all she wanted in the world was to close she eyes a second and rest sheself. And she *would* have too if only she'd been able, because those two eden-mangoes were calling out to her so loud and boisterous, she could never even close she eyes the stretch of a minute. Just the thought of that sticky, too-sweet orange flesh made she stomach turn inside-out nauseous again. But poor Moyen was *so* hungry, she could think of nothing else. She could only sit there in the grass staring at these two juicy mangoes holding in each of she hands, and after a time Moyen began to feel so sad and so desperate, that she began to cry. At last she decided to take just one little bite – just *one* – and she ripped off a strip of the rosy skin, swallowing down a mouthful of the dripping flesh.

Of course, after that first taste Moyen could never hold sheself back. She began to chew and suck and swallow as fast as she could manage, the juice dripping down she neck over she budding tot-tots, one fat mango and then the next. And of course, no sooner had all that too-sweet mango flesh filled up Moyen's little stomach, when she began to feel sick again, and it was all she could manage to crawl on she hands and knees to the side of the river, and vomit it all straight back up. Fortunate for Moyen the egg-shaped boulderstone of this woman was *up* river from where she vomited the mangoes instead of down, because there was no way to know how the woman would reprimand her if she saw all that nastiness floating past, and Moyen lay on she back on the cool grass beside the river. Dizzy and weak and so miserable, and at last she closed she eyes to cry sheself asleep.

But the woman appeared in no time a-tall to reprimand her anyway, not for all the vomit, because she gave Moyen a proper cursing when she found all the laundry already dry on the one side. Now Moyen hurried to turn all the clothes, and when everything was cripsy and dry, she helped the woman to fold it up. All the pillowcases and sheets and coverlets, the big white tablecloth and all the serviettes, and Moyen tied it all together in the big bundle. Now Moyen attended the woman to dress sheself, garment by garment, and she hurried to hoist the bundle up on top she head, stumbling behind the woman.

Only when they reached to the very top of the mountain, there before the tall iron gates at the entrance to that estate, did the woman turn around to address her again.

'Well Moyen,' she said, 'you are getting thinner! Tell me what is my name?'

Moyen could only stare down at the ground at she dusty feet. 'Miss Clementina?' she questioned.

'No!'

'Miss Dorothy?'

'No!'

'Miss Elizabeth-May?'

'No!'

The woman smiled again, she two hands poised on she hips, and she turned around again to walk in the direction of the big house.

Every evening it was the very same thing, the moment they reached to the tall, rusty gates:

'What is my name, Moyen? You are getting *thinner!*'

'Miss Josephine?'

'No!'

'Miss Mary?'

'No!'

'Miss Rosita?'

'No!'

And Moyen would look up at all those lovely, sickening eden-mangoes dangling from the tree just behind the gates. She would shake she head, and she would go to she bed hungry again.

Soon Moyen learned to wash the clothes every bit as well as the woman. She was just as careful, and she took the same pains with all the soaping and rinsing and the beating against the rocks. Now the woman had nothing to do a-tall, once she'd bathed sheself and rubbed she skin to glistening with the coconutoil, nothing but sit beneath the yellow poui beside the river and observe Moyen going about she labours. Soon the woman became so bored with sheself in truth – sitting there only waiting for lunch to come so she could wade up the river to she egg-shaped boulderstone – that that same day the woman decided to take the first of she lovers.

She pondered about it the whole night long, and the very next morning, as Moyen followed behind her toting the big bundle of laundry – just as they were passing the last little boardhouse of the village – the woman paused for a moment, and she entered into the shop of Mr Chan the Chinee grocer. She slipped she cutlass out from beneath she jackspaniard nest of hair, and she pointed it down at Mr Chan, sitting there on he little cedar-wood stool behind the counter. Mr Chan was at that very moment handing over a package of saltprunes he had just finished ringing on the register for Mistress Myrtle, but he jumped up straight away just the same. Mr Chan didn't even pause to lock the door of he grocery behind him! He took off hurrying before Moyen and the woman along the trace – with a little assistance from she sharp cutlass poking every few steps in he skinny yellow bamsee – straight to the banks of the river. Only when they reached did Mr Chan realize he was still clutching the cellophane package of saltprunes in he trembling hands. These he began now to eat, one after the next hurry hurry, because that was the only way he could think to calm he nerves, while Moyen assisted the woman to take off she clothes. And Mr Chan was still chewing the last of those saltprunes when the woman ascended the bank of the river again after she bath. Now, while Moyen busied sheself with all the washing, the woman directed Mr Chan to a private place beneath the huge banyan tree. There in a gully of moist leafy ferns, in the privacy beneath that banyan tree, the woman exercised Mr

57

Chan until it was time for lunch, and there wasn't a *single* jook remaining in he hard yellow bamsee! Of course, those three or four wadjanks fortunate enough to find theyselves hiding up at the top of that same banyan, were so distracted by this birds-eye view of all the pumping, and thumping, and boisterous ha-rumping going on below in the gully of soft ferns, that it was all they could manage to hang on tight with they left hand – while still taking good advantage of they right – and not tumble out the tree *bo-doops!* flat on top them.

The following morning, a Tuesday, the woman stopped at the house of Pierre the French tobacco-planter. Wednesday morning was Ram-sol, the Hindu roti-man. And Thursday morning was Orinoco, the Amerindian hunter from the rain-forests of Venezuela. Every day the woman chose a different race and ancestry, a different colour of skin, and texture of hair, and scent beneath they arms, so as never to become bored with sheself again, waiting beside the river for Moyen to finish the washing. And of course, just as you have already supposed – at the end of the week early on that Sunday morning – the woman didn't have no choice remaining but to slip she cutlass out from beneath she jackspaniard-nest of hair, and point it down at Ernesto, the Yankee tourist from the windy plains of Illinois. This Ernesto was an adventurer, a collector of all kinds of wild specimens from the tropical forest. So he brought with him he net, he tin of mosquito-spray and he tall rubber boots – he big magnifying glass and he bottle full to the brim with sugarcubes – only in hopes of capturing for heself the very rare blue-murmerer mariposa, and so to complete he collection. At least, that was he *intentions*. Until that fateful Sunday morning, when the woman waylaid Ernesto from he bright mariposas.

Of course, what the woman appreciated most about she vast

variety of lovers wasn't only the range and shape and size of they crab-os – that would be obvious enough – but in addition, she took a very keen interest in the particular *verbal* response each of them made at the moment of he greatest excitement. Because besides being what is sometimes referred to in the islands as a 'backyard-scientist', this woman was also a little bit of an apprentice *linguist* on top. So with all the dedication and control of a careful scientific investigation, she set sheself to discover the precise correlation between the two.

For example, Mr Chan the Chinee grocer. He had, just as you would expect, a corkscrew crab-o. And at the moment of he profound excitement he would bawl out a cry like a kung-fu fighter letting loose a series of chops:

ha-chong! ha-chong! ha-chong!

Felix the African fisherman, by contrast, had the most healthy specimen of them all. He crab-o would stand up tall and thick and very proud, and at the moment of *he* climax, he would let loose a series of deep solemn drumbeats. Just like he was back at home beating out a message on he conga:

bom! bom! bom! bom!

Clifton the English merchant, on the other hand, had a crab-o that curved hard to the right, and at the precise moment of *he* orgasm he would begin to giggle uncontrollable. Whereas Pierre the Frenchman curved radical to the left, and of course, at the moment of he supreme passion he would begin very sentimental to weep. Ram-sol the Hindu roti-man had a long thin crab-o reaching down between he knees, unless of course it was standing up almost to touch he nose, and he would let loose a deep

ommmmm!

just at the appropriate moment. Salman the Muslim of course had a crab-o much the same – except not so extreme in the length nor meagre in circumference – and just as you would expect, he would always offer up he prayer of thanksgiving:

ah-lah! ah-lah! ah-lah!

Orinoco the Amerindian hunter had a short thick crab-o with a wide girth like the ones you see in the paintings of Las Casas and the Spanish Captains, and at the height of he profound passion, he would let loose a bawl like a Warrahoon spying a quenk:

ay-ay-ay-ay-ay!

But the Yankee tourist from the windy plains of Illinois, this Ernesto, he had the saddest little crab-o of them all. Neither was it corkscrew, nor curving, nor short-and-thick nor tall-and-long. Neither was it pudgy, nor pickle-shaped, nor with a pointy head nor even a flat. On the contrary, the crab-o of this Ernesto was short and squat and very *scrawny*-looking, and to tell the truth, it put you very much in mind of the eraser end of a pencil! But this wasn't even the most peculiar trait of Ernesto the mariposa-collector. The funniest thing – and just the opposite of anything that you would expect – was that when *he* reached to the moment of he extreme excitement, instead of keeping he mouth shut considering especially the proportions of he little business, he would make more noise than all the rest together. And in the midst of a restful, peaceful Sunday morning! So much noise and confusion that the first time she heard it, the woman was afraid he'd burst the little purple vein at the side of he pencil-eraser. Just at the profound instant, just when you would expect him to hold he tongue, Ernesto would start up singing at the top of he voice – even to drown out all the hallelujahs of Jehovah the Almighty Conqueror just up the road – singing loud and patriotic for all the world to hear:

God bless A-mer-i-ca!
Land that I love!
Stand beside her!
And guide her!

and so on and so forth until the woman didn't have no choice a-tall but to quick scrape off a handful of moss from the bottom of the boulderstone beside her, and to stuff it inside he mouth!

Meantime poor little Moyen had scarce any chance to listen to all this singing. All this dramatic conga-beating, and praise-giving, and all the rest that was the pleasures of this woman, and she scientific-linguistic investigations. Moyen was much too busy beside the river struggling with all the clothes. And even if she *could* have listened with half-an-ear to all this confusion, she was far too distracted by the loud grumbling inside she own belly. All the time that Moyen was busy washing and tha wacking and fussing over all the laundry, she could think of nothing more than all those fruits on the estate that the woman wouldn't permit her to eat. All those pom-see-tays and pomeracs and barbadines. All the grapefruits and caimets and pinefruits, and on and on until she could no longer bear the pain in she belly, and she would begin again to cry. And it was late one afternoon, when she had finished scrubbing the clothes and spreading them all out on the grass – and she was waiting for them to dry with the woman and Mr Chan making every kind of obscene kung-fu chop in the gully with all the ferns – that Moyen became so sad and distressed, she began to wade up the river to escape all that terrible *ha-chung! ha-chung! ha-chung!*

Moyen climbed up to rest sheself on the big white boulderstone in the shape of an ostrich-egg, cool beneath the shade of the bois-cano. Of course, no sooner did she sit sheself down

61

when Crab-o appeared, side-stepping from out he hole beneath the rock. He sat there watching up at Moyen, and after a time he realized that the poor little girl was weeping. And of course, being as sensitive and tender of feelings as Crab-o was, in no time a-tall *he* started up weeping just the same. So there the two of them sat, tears rolling down they cheeks, until at last Crab-o raised he voice.

'Why are you crying little girl?' he asked her.

Moyen, of course, paid him no mind a-tall, knowing good enough – even in all she innocence – that crab-os can do plenty plenty things, but they can *never* talk.

'Tell me what is the matter,' he said again. And this time Moyen realized that it *was* Crab-o, in truth, who had spoken.

'Oh Crab-o,' Moyen sighed, 'you know the woman living in the big house up on top the mountain?' And Crab-o nodded his head. 'Well she won't give me none of the fruits of the estate unless I can guess she name, and I don't know she name, Crab-o. *Nobody* knows she name! I have asked in the village, I have asked all around, and nobody knows!'

Crab-o had already spied those two lovely eden-mangoes beside Moyen on the rock, because of course, that was *he* favourite fruit too. 'So what about those mangoes?' he asked her.

'Oh,' Moyen sighed again, 'I can't eat no more mangoes! That is the only fruit the woman would let me eat, and I have eaten *so* many mangoes, I feel to die!'

'Well,' Crab-o said sniffling still, 'you can dry you tears little girl. Because *I* will tell you the woman's name. But you can *never* tell her where you heard it from,' Crab-o warned. 'And you must be very careful, you mustn't guess it straight away!'

Now it was Moyen who nodded she head, and she offered Crab-o the two rosy mangoes.

'She name,' Crab-o said, raising he head up tall and smiling, 'is *Yan-killi-ma, Kutti-gu-ma, Yan-killi-ma, Nag-wa-kitti.*'

So Moyen, smiling sheself now for the first time in weeks and weeks, jumped down from the rock and hurried sheself back down the river. And that evening, when they reached to the top of the mountain at the end of the day, just before the tall iron gates, the woman turned around to face her again:

'You are getting *thinner*, Moyen! Tell me what is my name?'

This time Moyen put down the bundle of clothes she was toting on top she head. She paused a long minute, and she scrunched up she pretty little face like if she was concentrating good and hard. Then at last she answered:

'Miss Ruthy?'

'No!'

Moyen paused again. 'Miss Xena?'

'No!'

This time Moyen paused even longer. She shook she head again and again. At last she raised she big dark eyes to look up at the woman. 'I know what it is,' she said. 'It's *Yan-killi-ma, Kutti-gu-ma, Yan killi-ma, Nag-wa-kitti!*'

All in a sudden the smile disappeared from the woman's face. The burned saffron skin of she cheeks turned to a crimson brighter than those mangoes dangling from the tree above she head. All in a sudden the woman went vie-kee-vie in truth! She could never *believe* this child had guessed she name.

'I know who told you,' she bawled. 'I know who told you. *Crab-o* told you my name! *Crab-o* told you my name!'

And with that the woman pulled out the shiny cutlass from beneath she jackspaniard-nest – with Moyen thinking of course that she was coming after *her*, ready to turn quick and run for all she life – but the woman only passed her straight, continuing in a hurry on down the hill. Leaving Moyen there, of course, to eat any kind of fruit that she heart desired.

The woman walked all the way down to the banks of the river again. By that time twilight was just beginning to fall, turning the green river to a sheet of rippling gold. Crab-o had just finished consuming the very last morsel of sweet mango flesh. Because just like little Moyen, the first time *she* tasted those ripe juicy mangoes, Crab-o could never stop eating until he'd eaten them both, he belly ready to burst. Now he heard the woman singing again, as she came wading up the river toward the egg-shaped stone:

> *Crab-o, Crab-o*
> *Se-set-ou, dit-ou*
> *Ma-qua-nom!*

This of course was the local patois that Crab-o could understand as good as any of us. The woman was saying she knew perfectly well who had given away she name. So Crab-o was thinking to escape inside he hole first thing. But in truth he was feeling so full and lazy after eating those two huge mangoes, that he paused a moment to take in a deep breath and gather up he strength. By the time Crab-o saw the flash of the cutlass it was too late. Crab-o entered heself backwards inside he hole just like he always did, but he was so big and bloated after eating so much mango – so fat and chuff-chuff – that no matter *how* hard he pushed and shoved and strained, he could never fit heself back inside he hole. Still, he pushed and he shoved and he strained, struggling with all he strength to squeeze heself back inside. And in truth Crab-o managed – all except for he head – protruding out from the top of he hole.

With one quick slice of she cutlass the woman chopped it off! It was too late for Crab-o, there wasn't nothing he could do, and he had lost he head forever.

> *So the story goes*
> *Everybody knows*
> *Headless Crab-o stayed*
> *With only a back*
> *Crick-crack!*

64

❀

But this story is not yet finished as you might believe. Because even that revenge on Crab-o could never satisfy the anger of this woman. She remained sitting up in she bed the whole night stewing, beating she fist against the pillow and cursing, and next morning, a Monday morning, she was still in a terrible rage. Still vex and hot-up with sheself when Mr Chan appeared unsuspecting from behind he gru-gru bush, finishing off the last of he cellophane package of saltprunes – he crab-o standing up tall in the air with a big smile on he face – ready for he day of adventures. But Johnny, there wasn't no smile on the face of this woman a-tall. She took only *one* look – and without even pausing to consider the consequences – she slipped she cutlass out from beneath she jackspaniard-nest. In one clean swipe the woman decapitated the head of *he* crab-o too! All that remained of poor Mr Chan's crab-o was the skin wrinkled up at the end like a little turtle-neck jersey, with no head remaining to poke out from the neck a-tall!

Of course, the anger of this woman still had not subsided by the following morning, a Tuesday, and she performed the same unsuspecting decapitation on Felix the African fisherman. The next day was Wednesday, and it saw the beheading of the Englishman Clifton. Thursday morning was Pierre the Frenchman, Friday Ram-sol the Hindu roti-man, and Saturday of course was Orinoco the Amerindian hunter.

Even when Sunday morning arrived at the end of the week, the woman was still too vex to relax sheself. Ernesto the Yankee tourist appeared from behind he loveluck bush, wearing nothing a-tall but he tall rubber boots and a big smile on he face, he mariposa net and bottle of sugarcubes in each of he hands. The woman reached straight away for she cutlass, ready to perform the final beheading like all the rest. And she *would* have too – for a moment she even considered asking to borrow he magnifying glass so as to perform the operation proper – but the truth is that when she bent over to inspect he little pencil-eraser, poking out so sad between he two fuzzy quaileggs, something touched the heart of this woman. She realized, of course, that if she performed this final decapitation, poor Ernesto the mariposa-collector wouldn't have hardly nothing remaining of he little crab-o a-tall. It would be the same old story all over again of Hax the butcher, and in truth the woman could never live with that one on she conscience again.

Meantime Ernesto took only *one* glance at the face of this woman – not to mention she long silver cutlass raised high in the air, ready to swipe off its final decapitation! – and he dropped he net and he glassbottle of sugarcubes, he knapsack and all he mariposa-catching equipment the same instant. Instead, he grabbed on with both hands clutching tight to the *real* prize – which was nothing other than he scrawny little crab-o – and he took off running to catch the first American Airlines flight, straight back to the windy plains of Illinois.

That, of course, was a fortunate thing for us too. Even though of *all* the crab-os in all the world, the Yankee one is the only crab-o remaining with a head still poking out from its turtleneck jersey. Because despite that Ernesto didn't return to Illinois with he prize blue-murmerer mariposa as was he intentions, he brought back with him something of far greater importance. In *addition* to he little pencil-eraser: it is the very same tale that you have just finished hearing.

Johnny, you can finish the ending of this story just as easy as me. Because everybody knows that this Ernesto wasn't only a great adventurer, a collector of wild specimens from out the tropical forest, he was also a very famous American author too. And in time Ernesto wrote out this story of how he'd survived he adventure in the jungles of the savage Caribbean, without losing he head like all the rest. Of course, Ernesto could only relate it with all those same careful, real-life newspaper details that have become the trademark of all the famous Yankee writers. Including not only the precise proportions of he *own* little crab-o, but also the crab-os of Mr Chan the Chinee grocer. Of Orinoco the Amerindian hunter. He told them about Clifton the English merchant, and Pierre the French tobacco-planter. He painted out for them faithful word-pictures of the crab-os of Salman the Muslim, and Ram-sol the roti-man. And of course, he could never leave out the dangerous dimensions of Felix the African fisherman! To finish things off Ernesto gave he story a title with plenty intrigue and drama to make *sure* it would be a bestseller, even though he title, just like all he others, was exactly the *opposite* of what he tale was telling in truth: he called it *The Sad Story of the Savage American Practice of Circumcision.*

The result, Johnny, was everything that you would expect. And it has brought the biggest boom ever to we tourist industry. Because in no time a-tall the whole of America was telling this story too, even despite its confusing, backwards title. In no time a-tall even the travel brochures began to include – just beside the pictures of golden parrots, and green monkeys, and sparkling white beaches – precise descriptions of what, today, has become the most cherished of *all* we national treasures. Johnny, it is none other than you own decapitated Caribbean crab-o.

3

My Grandmother's Tale of the Kentucky Colonel and How They Made Their Fortune Selling Pizzas to the American Soldiers, Before Their Parlour was Raided by the Chief-of-Police for Prostitution and Illegal Trafficking

I tell you Johnny, when you are a young widow with a little bit of money and *plenty* good looks like I had in those days you've got to be careful, because it's only a set of men behind you, they want to rob you. The first was that same King of Chacachacari who tried to fool me with he story of buried treasure, that the only treasure I remained with was that gold brick there in the corner for the door not to bounce. And the second was the famous Kentucky Colonel – the same one of the fried chicken with he face painted on the pasteboard barrel, you know? – because he found heself here in Corpus Christi with the American soldiers, and the English, and all the rest of those scamps that descended like a hurricane on this island when they were fighting the war. But that was after it had been going for a few years already, and I'd moved out from the little house I had there on Mucurapo Road to the big one on Rust Street, and I fixed up the bedrooms nice that I could have five or six of those young American soldiers boarding with me. And those boys became like my own sons, all of them, and they used to pay me a few dollars each but *real* money, not those coconut dollars we had here then same as now, that they ain't even worth a fart.

So that morning I was there in the kitchen making the big pot of sancoche that my soldiers could have for they dinner, because *my* boys didn't want to hear nothing about no American cooking, nor English, nor Chinee nor nothing so – but only *West Indian* that was all they wanted to eat – which was fortunate for me also because that and few a Venezuelan dishes was the only kind I knew. I had just finished putting the remainder of the ground provisions and vegetables in the big pot to boil, when Amadao – he was only a youngboy twelve or thirteen years like you then – Amadao came running to tell me the Kentucky Colonel was waiting outside with he big white Cadillac motorcar parked up in front the house. So I asked Amadao *which* Kentucky Colonel did he mean, because I knew all the sergeants and lieutenants at the Base, and I even met the famous General Eisenhower, but I'd never heard nothing before about no Kentucky Colonel. Amadao said he wasn't the one of the Army, he was the one with the fried chicken that they called by the name of Colonel Sanders. *Well!* I started to get vex and I told Amadao to stop playing the fool, because that Colonel Sanders wasn't a *real* person, he was only the story those Americans thought up to sell they chicken – no different from the Uncle Sam in he big hat of the stars-and-stripes that they invented to sell the world they war – and I sent Amadao to tell whoever it was skylarking in front the house that if he didn't carry heself home, I would chop off he toe-tee and put it to boil with the rest of the carrots to make the sancoche!

But Amadao went and he came back again the next minute toting a dozen big white roses that he could scarce even see before him to walk, and he said the Kentucky Colonel sent these for 'Skip', and he was waiting outside for a little 'pow-wow'. So right away I knew it was one of my soldiers making sport with me this morning, just like they used to do all the time, because they were the only ones who called me by my namenick like that. You see, one thing I could never understand too good was those American soldiers when they came talking all they *twang*, and every time they said something I had to ask them to repeat it three and four different times. Most the time I *still* couldn't understand what the ass they were trying to tell me, so I just answered 'Skip it! Skip it, na man!' and that was how they put that namenick on me. So now I covered over the pot of sancoche, I fixed the roses in a big vase with water, and I went to the door to see which one of my youngboys was playing shitong on me this morning.

Johnny, when I reached at the door and I looked through the screen I nearly fell down, because sure enough parked right there in front the house was none other than the real life Kentucky Colonel! He was dressed up in he white suit with the little black ribbon tied in a bow around he neck for the tie, and the gold chain dangling from the vestcoat pocket – and he was sitting behind the wheel of he big white Cadillac motorcar with the roof which folded itself up and down – and all the chrome shining, and the fins and flippers and the wings pushing out from the two sides like a flyingfish jumping out the water. Sweet heart of Jesus! I had *never* in all my life seen nothing to compare with this big motorcar, not even the morning I jumped from my bed hearing this *voom voom voom* vibrating in the air like the world is coming to an end, and I ran in the yard to look up in the sky and see the Zeppelin!

So I could only think to quick take off the apron hanging around my neck, particular as right in front was a big green stain of sancoche, I fixed my hair a little bit, and I went outside to greet this Kentucky Colonel. Of course, by now there was a dozen little baboo-boys, and negritos, cocoa-pañols and all the rest screaming and sliding off the fins of this big motorcar, and sucking sweets that the Colonel gave them. But when they saw me they all quieted down straight away, and they made a space for me to approach the Colonel. But I could never know what was the proper etiquette for a Kentucky Colonel as I'd never met one before in my life, so I improvised a little curtsey with a wave of my hand and a sigh like if I was Scarlet sheself out the picture! Right away he told me, 'Skip' – and he took my

hand to plant a kiss wet on it with he pointy moustaches –
'Skip, tonight you and me got weself an appointment to *skin the
kitten!*'

But I could never understand the twang of these Americans
too good, and worst of all was the ones coming from the South,
so I told the Colonel how I already had the big skin of a tiger for
a blanket on my bed that I'd brought with me from Venezuela
especially as it was a gift from my great-uncle the famous General Francisco Monagas – so I wouldn't be needing for no kitten
that could scarce even make a pillowcase – and anyway I
wouldn't have no time tonight because I had to feed my soldiers they dinner. The Colonel said in that case we could
'hound the doggie' a little bit after supper. But I said I wouldn't
have time for none of that *hound-doggie* business neither, whatever the ass it was, because after dinner I was obliged to enter-
tain my boys by reading them the cards and telling them
fortunes and stories and sometimes we even had a little music
and dancing when the girls came around but I didn't permit
no nastiness! – because there were prostitutes enough in this
island since they started the war and turned it into nothing but
one big brothel to service all the soldiers, so he could go to one
of *those* houses if he was looking for *that!*

But now I watched the Colonel's face turn red red like if he
was insulted and he didn't take no for an answer. And now *I*
started to feel bad too – and I was thinking that in truth it's not
every day of the week that the real life Kentucky Colonel
arrives in front you house to pay a visit – so I told him he was
welcome to come tonight and take he dinner and entertainment
with me and my soldiers if he wanted. The Colonel smiled now
with he moustaches standing up straight in the air, and he said
in he twang, 'Skip, that would be dandy-randy!' and he let loose
a bawl like if he was John Wayne heself in one of those pictures
of the Wild West, '*Hee-hee-haw!*' Now he took off in he big white

Cadillac motorcar floating like the oceanliner down Rust Street, with five or six of those young baboos standing on the seat beside him, and some more in the back, and Amadao and all the rest running screaming in the dust like a tribe of jabmolassees behind the steelband on Jouvert morning!

So I stood there watching at all this commess until they disappeared around the corner, and then I went back inside to finish seeing about the sancoche. After a time Gregoria la Rosa arrived from market with a nice fat agouti, and she said she would add it to the pot. But now I stood there a moment studying Gregoria holding up this animal dangling by the tail – and smiling a big smile one ear to the next because for her, agouti was the *sweetest* meat in the world – when all in a sudden I realized that we could *never* feed this agouti to the Colonel Sanders. Because the truth, if you ever eat an agouti – despite that it is a great delicacy for any West Indian – the truth is that it's nothing more than an overgrown rat living in the forest. And even though I knew well enough my soldiers would think it a big big adventure that Gregoria and me have served them a rat to eat – and I could hear them saying already this was surely something to write home about – there was no way we could take the chance with this Kentucky Colonel who was bound to eat finicky finicky, as he didn't serve nothing in he restaurant more than frenchfries and fried chicken.

So Gregoria la Rosa and me began to discuss what we could serve to this Colonel Sanders, and she said of course that the only two things the Americans liked to eat are fried chicken and pizza. I told her that was obvious enough – and *I* wasn't about to try to compete with Colonel Sanders *heself* for he own fried chicken! – so the only choice remaining was to make the pizza. Of course, neither one of us had a clue what was the recipe for pizza, and when Gregoria told me that the only thing to do is for her to make a roti bread like the Hindus, and sprinkle some cheese and sausage on it that probably nobody wouldn't know the difference, now I realized that we were in big trouble in truth, and we could never accomplish this pizza without some help. But straight away I thought to send for Tony who was one of my boarders staying with me, because he was Italian coming from Little Italy in New York, where they say they eat plenty pizza, so maybe he could give us the recipe? So I called the special number my boys gave me that was the hotline to the Base that I must call it if I needed them in a hurry, and I told the soldier who answered to say to Tony that Skip had a *big big* emergency in the house, and he must come straight away!

Well, scarce had I put that telephone down when we heard the siren outside like the donkey braying with laryngitis, and the red lights on top the Jeep flashing. Next thing three soldiers came busting through the door with the gasmasks covering they faces, and the rifles firing *boo-doom! boo-doom! boo-doom!* with the crystals shattering in the chandelier above we heads – that Gregoria and me became *so* frightened all we could imagine was Hitler had arrived at last to invade the Caribbean just like the English promised us – and we buried weself trembling beneath the diningroom table! Just then one of the soldiers shoved he head under and took off he gasmask, and of course it was only Tony wanting to know what was this big emergency? *Well!* Gregoria and me were so startled we couldn't even catch we breaths to answer. They had to put us to sit down at the table and give us a tall glass of water each to drink, and then a little shot of whiskey to settle we nerves, before we could explain to them that the big emergency was the Kentucky Colonel coming for dinner tonight that all we could think to serve him was pizza, and we didn't know how the ass to make it.

Straight away the boys exclaimed, 'Oh, but you mean *that*

Kentucky Colonel!' and they chuckled a little bit, and Tony told us how the pizza wouldn't be no problem a-tall. He said how he had an Uncle Caesar in New York who was more famous for pizzas than anybody else alive, and how he had grown up *heself* making pizzas – or 'slinging pies', as Tony called them – almost before he could walk. Tony said too that the recipe for pizza was only a little flour and water and some tomato and cheese and sausage. But the important thing for a pie was not the ingredients – nor how much style nor fancy acrobatics you managed to sling it with – it was what kind of oven you baked the pie *in*. Tony said the best kind was a brick oven that cooked with logs of wood. But I said how were we to get a chance to build this big oven with bricks, because that Colonel was arriving for he dinner in only a few hours? But Johnny, right away I remembered the old rusty oven we used to have at the back of the yard in the little Mucurapo house – it was a kind of oven called a *Dutch* oven, that we were using them here to bake with before they brought all these fancy Westinghouse ones that cooked with electricity that half the time you didn't have none *anyway* – because sure enough that old Dutch oven baked with logs of wood. Only thing was, as I told Gregoria and the three boys, now that I'd sold the little house to the old Syrian, we had to go and thief that oven back.

You see, when Barto died leaving me in this big big house, I said that I didn't want to be in here no more a-tall. Because this house had so many bedrooms and bathrooms and you uncles Rodolfo and Reggie both ready to leave for Canada to study medicine anyway, with José and Paco soon to follow behind, and both the girls Inestasia and Elvirita already married-off too. So I decided to move back to the little house on Mucurapo where you daddy and Amadao both were born, because I

74

loved that little house so much. And I did just that, and I put the big house to rent with a rich Syrian, and it was that money that went to feed the children and sustain us all together. But then when the war started and already I had the four boys in Canada that I had to be sending them money all the time, I decided the only thing to do was to sell the big house to the rich Syrian, especially as Barto built it for only seven-thousand dollars and this Syrian wanted to give me *twenty*.

But as fate would have it I had put an oldwoman by the name of Mrs Carmichael to live in the basement of this house even before the Syrian moved in, and that was the only reason I was feeling a little bit bad to sell it, because I would have to tell her to leave. The funny thing now was that even before I had a chance to tell her anything, one morning straight out the blue she came to me and she said, 'Mrs Domingo, I never met you husband before in my life, but last night I had a vision with him and he said to tell my wife she can *not* sell this house. It's the little house on *Mucurapo* she has to sell to the Syrian, and move back inside the big one here.' *Well!* I didn't know what to think except maybe this oldwoman didn't want to leave, and so she made up all this business about the vision with Barto to try and trick me. But when I asked her how Barto looked, that maybe I could catch her up in a good boldface lie, she told me she didn't have a clue. What Mrs Carmichael said was that the only thing she saw of Barto was he *toes*. That she was lying in she bed saying she chaplet as usual when she smelled this smell of fresh-picked strawberries, and when she raised she eyes from she chaplet, Barto's feet were standing right there at the foot of she bed. And she said how those toes were the most *beautiful* things she had ever seen in all the world – long and white with the toenails pink pink at the ends like a bowl of strawberries and cream fit for the Queen sheself in Buckingham Palace to eat them – *so* beautiful she could never look up from them to see Barto's face, because all she wanted to see for the rest of she life were those toes and weep. So straight away I knew to believe *everything* this oldwoman told me – because Barto was a handsome man in truth – but one thing for sure he had the most beautiful feet in all the world, just like a young-girl's own that never put on no shoes in she life harder than silk Chinee slippers.

So that same afternoon I went with Mrs Carmichael to tell the Syrian how I had changed my mind and I couldn't sell him that house, not even for twenty-thousand dollars. Well the Syrian got *vex*, and he started to curse me up and down, but I told him I didn't care that if he wanted he could have the little house on Mucurapo for half the money. And that was just what happened. The rich Syrian and me exchanged houses, and Mrs Carmichael remained there just where she was, so now all in a sudden I found myself in this big empty house with all these bedrooms and bathrooms, with me dragging my feet from one to the next all the day and night. But I didn't worry too much, and every time I started to feel a little bit sad about those twenty-thousand I'd given up I went downstairs for Mrs Carmichael to tell me about Barto's toes again, and the cream and strawberries for the Queen in Buckingham Palace, because that was the only thing to give me a little hope.

And I hadn't been there in Rust Street more than a couple months when all in a sudden one afternoon I got the call from Sergeant Warren at the American Base! What he told me was that they had selected a few prominent widows of the island that I had come to them very very *highly* recommended, and Sergeant Warren wanted to know if I would consider taking in for boarding a few boys, five or six or as many as I could handle. He said that the American Army would *guarantee* the payment of each one of these boys in American dollars, plus ten-thousand *more* dollars that they would pay me on top to get the house ready for them. *Papa-yo!* Ten-thousand *Yankee* dollars, not the coconut ones, that of course I grabbed up that money and I ran to hide it straight away in the bank, because all I had to do to make the house ready for these boys was sweep out the rooms a little bit and make the beds. And Johnny, it was those ten-thousand that went to support you uncles in Canada studying medicine, plus the little money that the soldiers were paying me every week, and don't forget about the other ten-thousand coconut dollars that the Syrian gave me too. But of course, when I sold that little house I never thought to take the rusty old Dutch oven with me, because how could I ever imagine that one day I would need it to cook the Kentucky Colonel he pizza?

So we went downstairs to see Mrs Carmichael, Tony and me and the two boys, because she'd lived with that rich Syrian all these years, and she would know what was the best way to get that Dutch oven back. I suggested maybe we could pay one of the girls from Point Cumana a few dollars so she could distract the Syrian while me and the two boys sneaked around the side of the house and thiefed the oven? But this Mrs Carmichael only started to giggle like if somebody was tickling her down below there, and she said the most *expensive* prostitute in the whole of Point Cumana could never distract that old Syrian for even a second, as everybody but Skip knew he was the biggest buller on the whole island! Of course, Tony and the two boys could never understand *we* island slang now – and plus they were soldiers of the American Army that so far as me and Mrs Carmichael could only *imagine*, they wouldn't know nothing about this nastiness neither – and they wanted to know what do we mean to say the Syrian was an old *buller?* Well, Mrs Carmichael smiled and she said *Mary*, and I smiled and said *jump-over-the-fence*, and Mrs Carmichael said *softman*, and I said *borrow-the-Bishop's-crosier*, but still these boys couldn't understand what we were trying to tell them a-tall. All in a sudden Tony's eyes lit up like the jabjab had jumped inside he skin in truth, and he jumped up on top Mrs Carmichael's coffeetable, he dropped he khaki soldier pants and underneath was a frilly pink panties that could rival any *one* of those girls at the Point, and he began to shake up he little white bamsee with these two boys whistling away! Tony began singing in he American twang the famous calypso that everybody was singing that year, and he was dancing just like this:

> *Rum and coca-cola*
> *Down to Point Cumana,*
> *Mothers and they daughters*
> *Working for the Yankee dollar!*

Ayeeyosmío! Johnny, I'd better sit down quick before I fall *boodoops!* on the ground. What a thing eh, when you get old? To think that only a few centuries ago I used to dance them all into the dust. And look at me now! But the hips could still wind a little bit, and the bamsee could still shake, and the legs are not so bad for an oldwoman that needs this cane to walk with. Even though half the time I forget it and I have to send one of you running to my room to fetch 'my husband', which is how I call it. In truth, this cane is the best kind of husband for an oldwoman like me, because even at the age of ninety-six I *still* haven't given up hope that one morning I might wake up and need him, *papa-yo!*

So where I was now? Oh yes, so Tony informed us that not only was he the most famous pie-slinger in the whole of New York and America too, he was also the most popular of *all* the burlesque dancers in a big theatre they had on Time Square called the *Playhouse. Well!* poor old Mrs Carmichael near pitched down in a faint, and me behind her, but when we recovered weself we said that in truth, the best plan was for Tony to distract the Syrian with he burlesque dance and he little pink panties, and in the mean time me and the two boys would sneak around the house and thief that old Dutch oven before the Syrian could even realize what hit him!

Of course, old Mrs Carmichael said she wanted to see this thing too – that she wouldn't miss it not even for Mass on Corpus Christi Day – and Gregoria la Rosa, that in the end all *six* of us went together to Mucurapo and we hid behind the bushes looking in through the window. Well, everything worked perfect just as we had planned. Tony jumped up on top the coffeetable and dropped he khaki pants and started to jiggle he little bamsee in he frilly pink panties – with that old Syrian staring so hard he eyes swelled out like a sapo's own – when all in a sudden I looked around for those *other* two soldiers because now was the perfect time to grab up that oven and make we get away, but they'd both flat disappeared! Next thing we saw was both those other two boys up on top the coffeetable all *three* of them jiggling they little white bamsees in they frilly pink panties – and then the old Syrian with he fat pumpulum and he big baggy drawers dragging-down up on top the table jiggling *too!* – that poor old Mrs Carmichael and me and Gregoria la Rosa were so scandalized by this thing, we almost fell down dead with a heart attack one after the next behind them bushes! It was all we could manage to drag that rusty old oven around the house, and we strained weself to tumble it in the back of the Jeep. Now I put on the siren braying *he-haw he-haw he-haw* like the donkey with laryngitis again, and the red lights on top flashing – with me behind the wheel and Mrs Carmichael and Gregoria la Rosa holding on for dear life – and we took off as fast as that Jeep could carry us away from this orgy of bullers going on inside the house!

Of course, Tony and those two boys could never reach home until five minutes before the Colonel was due to arrive for he pizza, all with they faces smiling ear-to-ear and red like three roukous after all they exercise and excitement. So it was a good thing Gregoria and me already had that Dutch oven in the backyard prepared with the logs of fire flaming, and let me tell you by this time *I* was flaming too! But Johnny, when I stood there in my own backyard to watch at Tony slinging the dough for this pizza – spinning it on one finger up over he shoulder, back behind he back, down beneath he leg throwing it spinning up in the air high as the sapadilla tree to catch it on the same finger spinning again – *well!* I quick forgot all that nastiness going on with the old Syrian. I could only stand there beside Gregoria and Mrs Carmichael the three of us *mesmerized* like three chupidees, only watching at Tony slinging this pie. I told him that in truth if he wasn't such a buller and so much like my own son to me, *I* would have married him right there on the spot only for him to serenade me in the sunset every evening for the rest of my days by slinging out a pie! Now Tony prepared the dough with the tomato and cheese and sausage, and he said that Dutch oven was the perfect thing to cook this pizza. And Johnny, when this pizza-pie came out from that oven with the crust cripsy cripsy, and the cheese bubbling and the sausage and everything – and Tony divided it up to give us each a test slice to taste – we all said that it was the most *delicious* thing we'd ever eaten in all we life. Even *Mrs Carmichael* said how wonderful, never mind she could only suck the crust a little bit as she didn't have not a tooth in she mouth left to chew it.

So now I started to relax myself for the first time since the Kentucky Colonel arrived that morning, and I said there wasn't *nothing* better for us to serve him than that pizza. And after a few minutes he pulled up in the drive with he big Cadillac motorcar still loaded down with all these little boys, and sitting beside him smoking he cigar was he partner who had come all the way from Australia to fight in the American Army, and the Colonel introduced him to me as the *Tanzanian Devil*. So I made my little curtsey like Scarlet again for this Tanzania, and I said how he was welcome to come inside and take he pizza with me and all my soldiers, but *not* all this amount of baboos that they must remain outside in the Cadillac motorcar, and Tony will send a next pie for them.

So we all went and sat weself around the big diningroom table, and Tony brought in the first pie that was a plain one with only cheese and tomato on it. Gregoria and the two boys served a round of cerveza, because of course that is the only suitable thing to drink with pizza. Well, the Colonel spread he serviette careful around he little potbelly, and he said how pizza was he favourite thing to eat in all the world – that he was so tired eating frenchfries and fried chicken all day, every day, morning noon and night he had them up to he catfish-whiskers – and when he had a taste he said how Tony's was the *best* he'd ever tried. Even Tanzania said how that pie was first-rate – but what had he mouth watering most of all were those rosy ripe julie-mangoes for dessert – and with that he reached out he two hands to give Gregoria's tot-tots a squeeze. Sweet heart of Jesus! Gregoria let loose a cry and she dropped the pizza she was carrying to take off running for the kitchen, and straight away I advised this Tanzania he'd better behave heself and mind he manners, or there wouldn't be *no* more pizza for nobody a-tall. And with that I took out my little pearlhandled pistol from between my own tot-tots, and I rested it down on the table to let him know I meant business too!

Now they brought in a pepperoni pie and a next one with

onions and black olives, and of course we had to drink a next round of cerveza. Of course, we sent a pie outside too for those little boys waiting in the Colonel's motorcar, and a round of coca-colas. Then they brought in a next pie for us and this one had a fried egg floating in the middle of it, and swimming all around in the tomato sauce was the little anchovy fish, and of course we had to drink a next round of cerveza. Next we ate a pie with mushrooms, then one with green peppers, then another one with rings of pineapple and bacon on it. And just when we thought we were all going to *die* if we ate another slice of pizza, another sip of cerveza, Tony brought in a next *deluxe* pie that he said was he *speciality*, and this one had on it all the other ingredients of all the other previous pizzas piled up together – tomato and cheese and onions and black olives, green peppers and mushrooms and pepperonies and pine-apple and bacon, three different fried eggs, with a *sea* of anchovy fish drowning beneath – so of course we couldn't *help* weself but try a next little slice each of Tony's speciality pizza, and of course more cerveza. Johnny, let me tell you pizza was pizza-*pie* that we ate that evening with the Kentucky Colonel, that when we were finished we could only sit there groaning with all we bellies bloat-o beyond belief – with every now and then a belch from so much cerveza foaming – and the Colonel excused heself to press he little round potbelly and pass a fart for all those pepperonies.

But after a time we all recovered weself, and just like every night when dinner was finished the boys begged me to tell them a story. Straight away they started to fight down each other about which one it would be tonight – the story of the man with he toe-tee that wouldn't go down for three years and three-hundred women before he met the Mother Superior Maurina, or the one of Mrs Wong and she sideways pussy, or the story of that same pearlhandled pistol there on the table

82

and the tiger that liked to eat cheese – and *all* the old stories that were all they favourites. But I told them that they would have to wait until tomorrow as I was too tired especially after this big marathon of eating pizza, and in any case the Colonel was we guest of honour tonight that we didn't want to bore him with none of those old bedtime stories. But the Colonel stood up straight away to beat he spoon against he glass still foaming with cerveza, and he make a big speech to say how he had *never* received such hospitality like this south of the border before, and it would be he great *privilege* tonight to hear the mistress of the house relate one of she famous tales! With that all the boys started to shout and whistle and clap they hands together that of course I had to oblige them, and I went on to relate a short one that is called

The Tail of the Boy Who Was Born a Monkey

You see, there in Estado Managas in Venezuela where I was living they had a family and the little daughter took in sick, and she was sick a long long time that they didn't know what to do for her. But the family had money, so they took the girl to the English doctor trained in *England* by the name of Dr Rubies Wilson, and this doctor examined the girl and he said there was only one thing that would cure you daughter. Dr Rubies said they must give her some monkey blood to drink. But he warned them they had to kill the monkey *fresh*, and take out that blood straight away, and give it to the daughter to drink. So the father paid a man to go with him on this excursion in the jungle to shoot this monkey. But the wife of the man now, the mother – she was a youngwoman just like *you* mummy there in the photograph on top my bureau – she said how she wanted to go in the jungle with them. But the thing that nobody didn't know was that this woman was pregnant, *just* pregnant – because even *she* didn't realize it yet – otherwise they would *never* have allowed her to go with them to shoot this monkey.

So all three of them went together on this hunting excursion inside the jungle. And when the rifle fired so – *paps!* – and they shot the monkey, they all saw now that the monkey had a little baby, and she had it cradling in she arms sucking tot-tot *slup-slup-slup* just like a real baby. Now the monkey raised up she baby in the air, to *show* them, and she said '*ee-ee-ee!*' as if to say, 'Look, *I* have a baby too!' Well, the woman was standing there watching this thing, and when the monkey dropped down dead she got *vex*. She cursed them up and down and she said you have committed a crime, you have killed the mother of this poor monkey! *She* took that baby monkey up, and she carried him home, and she cared for him. And the father took the blood and gave it to he daughter to drink, and of course the little girl was cured now and she get better in no time a-tall.

Everybody was thinking this was the end of the story, but this story was not finished yet. You see, the woman grew to love she baby monkey very much, and she cared for him and raised him up – and some people used to say she fed him with she *own* tot-tots – but I knew it was not true, that these people only became confused by what happened *after*. She used to feed him with a little bottle, just like a real baby, and she dressed him up in the little diapers and carried him around hanging from she neck and riding on top she head wherever she went. But then one day when the woman wasn't watching the monkey jumped through the window, and he disappeared back inside the jungle.

Well, the woman grew *distressed* from this thing, she loved this baby monkey so much, and now she said she wouldn't accept no baby that was not a monkey. Of course, the husband was distressed too, just as you could imagine. Because by now

84

the woman was big big out to here with they *second* child –
remember how I told you that all this time the woman was
pregnant? – and she was only saying now how she wouldn't
accept no baby that was not a monkey. The husband was *so*
upset that he went to consult with all the doctors, Dr Rubies
and all of them, but they all said the same thing that there
wasn't nothing to do, only wait and we will see.

And those doctors were right! Because when the baby was
born sure enough he come out with the tail of a monkey – the
tail *only* – but that tail was enough to satisfy this woman and
make her love the baby just as much as the one that she had
lost, and the father too. It was a *real* monkey tail, long and curling with a tuft of hairs at the end, with this baby swinging on
he tail from the bars of he crib crying '*ee-ee-ee!*' all the time just
like he mummy. And you couldn't cut those hairs on that
baby's tail! Because one time the father held down he son and
he tried to cut those tail-hairs, and the wife got so vex she went
behind *him* with the scissors! It's a true story Johnny, because I
saw this child myself. They called him *The Boy Who Was Born a
Monkey*, and they painted a sign to say it too, even though it
was a little bit dishonest because the only thing he had was the
tail. They used to make money with him on the wharf, and take
out photographs with the tourists when they came in off the
big ship, and they made a little pants special with a long sleeve
behind for that tail to fit perfect inside.

Well! we were all so involved in this story now we didn't even
realize what was happening beneath we own narices – and that
is the sure sure danger when it comes to telling stories – that
sometimes you lose track of you *own* harsh reality you're living. Because before this story could even reach its happy ending, we heard one set of bawling coming from inside the

kitchen. Now we took off running to find poor Gregoria on she back on top the counter with all she skirts up around she waist – and all those dirty plates with the curls of pizza crust, and tomato sauce, and half-drunk bottles of cerveza – with this pendejo Tanzania sprawled out on top trying he best to shove he nasty toe-tee inside. Sweet heart of Jesus! I grabbed up he cojones in my fist and I squeezed them tight – and I said how it was a lucky thing for him I forgot my pearlhandled pistol there on the table – and if he didn't get heself down from that counter this instant I would *rip* them out by they *roots*, and I would pelt them so far away he would have to look by *Australia* to try to find them! Of course, my boys were there beside us and they all loved Gregoria and me like if we were both mothers to them, and they held on to this Tanzania to carried him outside and put one set of blows on him like pepper!

All I could do was to take up poor Gregoria in my arms and try my best to console her, and in no time a-tall she recovered sheself. Of course, the Colonel had to come begging me on he *knees* please to tell my boys to spare he partner Tanzania, because if I didn't call them off they would kill him for sure. I told him he should have thought about that before he brought this wadjank inside the house that he didn't have no manners nor respect for the people – and I didn't care if it was Tanzania, or Transylvania, or *Timbucktoo* he came from he had to behave heself – and I told the Colonel that I would call my boys off but only if he promised to pack up heself and he partner in they big white motorcar, and they can never show they faces in this house *never* again! So the Colonel took off and everything quieted down, and my boys came back inside and we were all there in the kitchen helping Gregoria to clean up after this big commess, but I was still so vex I declared a *moratorium* on pizzas in the house until the war finished, if any of us could ever live to see *that* happy end!

Of course, first thing the following morning just as you have already guessed, there was this Colonel and he Tanzanian Devil parked up again in front the house, and they sent Amadao toting a dozen white roses for *Gregoria* this time. Amadao told us how Tanzania sent to offer he profoundest apology – how he suffered from a rare condition very common in he country, that even the *smell* of an anchovy fish made he crowbar to stand up stiff like iron, and he didn't have no choice but to pry-open something with it – and did we mind if he and the Colonel came in for only a minute, as they had a very important business proposition for the two ladies of the household. *Well!* I told Amadao to tell that Tanzania and he Colonel we don't want no business to do with them a-tall, and I advised Gregoria that if she knew what was good for sheself, she would pitch those fucking flowers first thing in the sea. But Gregoria was only skipping around the kitchen smiling like a little girl with a spider crawling inside she panties, and she told me today was the first day in all she life that she felt worthy of she namesake, because nobody had never given her no flowers before, not even the blossoms of a stinking-toe bush. *Ayeeyosmío!* I didn't have no choice a-tall, and I said it was up to Gregoria – that if she wanted to invite those two scoundrels back inside the house she could – but don't blame *me* for the consequences.

So Gregoria brought them inside again and we put them to sit in the livingroom, and the next thing I saw was a little hand reaching out to the Colonel from behind the sofa. Then I saw Amadao take off running out the door bawling

'*Fakee fakee pudinum bakee!*'

and I had to call him back and reprimand him to please give the gentleman back he moustaches. Now Gregoria asked Tanzania if she could offer him a coffee, 'or some other nice little refreshment' – and she had she eyelashes beating for him like a battimamselle – but the Colonel answered straight away that they wouldn't have time for none of those little pleasures until later, because they had *plenty* preparations to get the house ready tonight for the grand opening of

Skippy's Pizza Parlour

Oui fute, papa-yo! I informed this Colonel and he devil Tanzania how I had declared a moratorium on pizzas in this house after all that nastiness of last night, and I let them know without no questions about it that this was a respectable boarding house for the soldiers of Uncle Sam and *He* American Army – it was not a parlour for pizzas, nor prostitutes, nor fried chicken nor nothing else – and I made it clear in capital letters that Gregoria and me didn't have NO interest in they business proposition A-TALL!

But when I looked around for Gregoria to corroborate with me on this big speech, I saw now she wasn't even *listening* – she was perched there in the corner sitting on the lap of that Tanzania like a little purple finch – and from the smile on she face and the squirm of she waist it was obvious enough to me she perch wasn't exactly a *twig!* And now I studied the profile of this Tanzania a moment and I realized for the first time that he was a *handsome* devil in truth, and how Gregoria and me were *both* in hot water with these two men up over we heads! On top of all that I suppose this predicament had me a little bit nervous, since just as always when I am nervous I said the first thing to come inside my head – and of course it was the *worst* possible thing – because now I asked this Colonel what did he have in mind for he pizza parlour?

The Colonel informed me how the Americans only liked to eat two things that are fried chicken and pizza – and just like Gregoria the day before I said yes, that is obvious enough – and how he *already* had the fried chicken market sewn up tight as the culo of a pavo with he Kentucky restaurant there beside the

88

Base. 'But,' said this Colonel, 'that leaves wide open and ready for us to exploit the entire *pizza* market! And with all those Americans living on the Base, and with so many more still to come – and with all the natives of this island of course mimicking the Americans, or the English or French or whoever-the-ass other foreigners arrived here quick as monkey-see-monkey-do – in no time we will all be *multi-multi-multi*-millionaires with this pizza parlour!' The Colonel said how I would soon be the *Queen of Pizzas* for the entire Caribbean, and Gregoria la Rosa my *Princess in Waiting*, 'easy as plucking a couple of juicy ripe Georgia peaches fresh out they panties'!

So I told the Colonel how everything he said was obvious enough – but in truth I have never been a millionaire in all my life, and I don't want to be a millionaire – but then again that business of the Queen and she Princess in Waiting *did* sound to me a little bit appealing. The problem, as I explained to the Colonel, was that Gregoria and me already had we hands full with all the work of running this boarding house for the soldiers, so how could we *possibly* find time to run this pizza parlour on top? Now the Colonel asked me if it wasn't obvious *he* was the expert when it came to fastfood? – and I said yes, that was obvious too – so therefore he and he partner would provide the labour force and handle all the preparations. Gregoria and me would be the two *hostesses* of this parlour. Therefore we wouldn't have nothing to do but stand there beautiful and smile for the boys – or show them to the toilet or a back-bedroom if they needed to take care of some unforeseen necessity in a hurry – and maybe we could also get the logs in that Dutch oven going when the time came. The Colonel said too how he'd arranged everything with Tony and the two boys, and they were already dispatched to prepare all the pizzas.

But Johnny, something about this Colonel had me a little bit suspicious – particular when I looked at those catfish-whiskers

that were stuck on now upside-down – so I said that I would
have to think about this thing good and weigh up all the consequences, and now I turned to Gregoria again to ask her what
did *she* have to say about this business venture? But Johnny,
when I looked in the corner where Gregoria was perched on
the lap of this Tanzania, I found the two of them giggling-away
like two wicked schoolchildren – and Tanzania had poor Gregoria's blouse unbuttoned down to she midriff – and he was
tickling her with one of those *same* fucking white roses, all the
way down between she tot-tots. Sweet heart of Jesus! When I
saw this thing going on in the corner like that I became all distressed. Because even though Gregoria was a grown woman
now and she could handle sheself – I knew good enough that
she was *no* match a-tall for a handsome devil like this Tanzania
– because in truth I knew her better than anyone, since it was
me who gave Gregoria she name and raised her up from a little
girl as I loved her so much.

The Story of How Gregoria la Rosa Got She Name

You see, the story goes that when we first came to this island
from Venezuela they had a little village by the name of Paria up
in the mountains of the north coast. And living in this village
were the last people of Carib blood – that is to say, *indios indigi-
nos* – the very last ones remaining on the whole island, but of
course by this time they were mixed with African blood too.
There were only seven of them, a single family, when a sickness
came that they didn't know what it was – yellow fever, or
malaria, smallpox or something so – and it started to kill them
off one by one. *Quick*, because before the week could finish all of
them were dead. Well nobody didn't want to do nothing about
this tragedy. They didn't even want to *bury* them, the govern-

ment people – because of course at that time in this place they didn't know *who* the government was – if it was Spain, or England, or France or what. So I told my husband that this thing was a *scandal*. I told him *I* was going to bury them! And that was just what I did, and I paid a man to make the six boxes each one a different size for each member of the family, because we didn't even know about this little girl yet. We buried them right there in the little cemetery beside the village where they were living. But then after we finished burying them Barto went with me inside the thatched ajoupa house, typical for those Indians, because I told him I wanted to see it. I didn't know why, I just had this feeling – that *something* was there inside that little house – but I didn't know what it was.

Barto and me were just about to leave when we heard a soft noise in the corner, and when we turned around we saw, there in one of those little hammocks – they call them chicoros, the hammocks of those Indians – there in that little hammock was this child, and she was only crying crying for she mummy that she had lost. And Johnny, when I saw this little girl abandoned there like that, my heart broke in truth! She was no more than two-three years of age, and she was sick, very sick – like she didn't have no *blood* inside – because she skin had the colour of a yellow pawpaw. So I told Barto we had to take care of her. *I* would take care of her. And we held on each to an end of that same little hammock, and we carried her like that all the way home, with this little girl crying crying the whole way for she mummy. Now I said to Barto that we had to do something for this child because she was so sick, and we sent for all the doctors to come and examine her, but they didn't know what the sickness was, and they all said she would die. All I could think to do was to rub her down with sweetoil to try and soothe she yellow pawpaw skin, and we tied the little hammock up in the corner of we bedroom, and Barto tied a string to he foot that he could rock her in the night when she started to cry.

It was the old African woman that used to come to visit sometimes at the house – a woman by the name of Mrs Beulah – it was this oldwoman who cured the child and gave her back she blood. Mrs Beulah saw how I was in such a state of distress over this child, and she told me, 'Don't worry, Mrs Domingo! *I* going to cure her. I going to give her a dose of casteroil first to purge her, and then I going to make something.' She made a thing from aloes, and she chopped them up and put them with camomile – and some little root that I didn't know what it was – and guanabana, that we used to make icecream, and she put everything together in a big pot to boil. Then she let it cool, and she strained it out through a cloth inside a big jar, and she tied this jar hanging from a tree outside in the yard, that it could get sun and dew. At first it had the colour of piss, this thing, but after seven days it turned to a deep, rosy-purplish kind of colour.

Mrs Beulah said *good*, and she took a little cup and made the child drink some. She didn't want to drink it, but Mrs Beulah made her take a little cup every morning. And in *seven* days this child changed from that same colour of piss – that colour of a yellow pawpaw – and she turned to the same rosy-purplish colour of those roses they have climbing on the walls in Spain, because when I went on my pilgrimage to Lourdes I saw them, and they are the most *beautiful* kind of flower! That is how I named her: Gregoria la Rosa. And she grew up into a woman *just* as beautiful as she name!

She grew up with all of us, and she learned to speak we language and she went to school, and when she finished school she said she didn't want to take no job. She wanted to stay right there in the house and help me mind the boys. And when the boys grew up and they all left to study in Canada, and I decided to move back into the little house on Mucurapo, she said she wanted to go back and live in she little village of Paria by the sea. Especially as it was a big town now with a movie theatre and shopping centre and everything. But Gregoria told me that if I *ever* needed her to help in the house again, only to send word. So when I moved back to Rust Street and I made the boarding house for all the soldiers, first thing I sent for Gregoria and she came straight away, next morning, with the two of us only hugging up each other and crying and laughing at the same time like if we were mother and daughter in truth!

So when I looked around now to see this Tanzania making such a *fool* of her with that flower tickling down between she tot-tots, and a next one biting like a flamenco dancer between he teeth, I felt distressed, and nervous, and all I could think was how I wanted that Tanzania and he Colonel out of my house that very *instant!* And just as always when I am nervous I said the first thing to come inside my head, and just as always it is the worst *possible* thing, because now I said to that Colonel, 'Didn't you tell me how you and Tanzania had plenty preparations to get ready tonight for the grand opening of Skippy's Pizza Parlour?'

Now they took off in they big car, and I gave Gregoria a good long lecture first thing, that she must be *very* careful with a good-looking man like that Tanzania. Especially with a big handful like he had because come to think of it my fist couldn't scarce fit around them, and that was the *first* thing to give them a swelled head! Gregoria told me not to worry myself. She said how she had plenty of experience with men more dangerous than this Tanzania. That he ain't nothing more than a little puppydog licking between she ankles, and as soon as she could take him for all he was worth and have some good sport for sheself at the same time, she would send him packing. Gregoria persuaded me with such confidence that she could handle this Tanzania, that I didn't worry about him, nor the Colonel, nor they pizza parlour for the whole remainder of the day.

And it was not until late that afternoon that the Colonel arrived at last in he Cadillac motorcar – only written out now across the lengths of both the fins at the sides was

Skippy's Pizza Parlour – Free Delivery!

and following behind him in a big Army jitney all painted in the colours of camouflage, was he partner the Tanzanian Devil. So Gregoria and me stood up now to watch at Tanzania unloading this jitney, with the Colonel talking a mile a minute giving he orders left and right. Just there beside the Dutch oven in the backyard, before we could even blink we eyes twice, Tanzania erected a green Army tent big as the three-ring circus of Bailey and Barnum! Beneath it was a set of long wood tables, and wood benches, and then they began to unload all the stacks upon stacks of tin plates – each one stamped out the same *Property of the US Army* – the buckets of knives, forks, spoons, and a big roll round as the Colonel heself of paper serviettes. Now on the other side of that Dutch oven the Colonel planted a big banner blowing in the breeze, that it was the first thing to make any sense to me in all this confusion descending so sudden to take over we lives, and it said

Portable Mess

I told Gregoria that with this big tent and the tables and benches, at least we wouldn't have those soldiers traipsing through the house to dirty it up. Gregoria said yes, and another good thing was the roll of paper serviettes and the buckets of knives and forks and all the stacks of tin plates, because at least now they wouldn't be soiling and breaking up all we Castleford chinas, and flatwares, and clean linens. Gregoria and me were so impressed by everything we couldn't *help* but tell the Colonel how we never in all we life imagined so much fancy style only to sell a few pizzas, and we certainly hoped he could sell some after all he expenses and effort. The Colonel said not to worry about nothing – that there ain't *no*body in the world who knows the business of fastfood better than him – and I said yes, *that* is a fact! Now he took us around to the front of the house to show us the sign Tanzania had installed, but when we looked in the front yard we didn't see nothing a-tall. The Colonel only laughed and he told us to lean we heads back and look up in the sky – and when we did we near tumbled over backwards – because sure enough stretching all the way across the roof in those tall curling letters of neon lightbulbs was

Skippy's Pizza Parlour – Free Delivery!

just like he car, with my *own* telephone number in tall red digits blinking below. *Well!* we could only tell the Colonel again how impressed we were with everything, and we hoped he could sell a pizza or two. The Colonel said again not to worry about nothing, only to go and get weselves all dolled up in we finest with the jewels glittering on we 'bountiful boozooms' – because that was how he called tol-tols in he Southern twang – and Gregoria and me said that was *exactly* what we were going to do!

But Johnny, when we turned around to go inside the house we near stumbled flat on top we faces, because just there before the front door was a tall stack of twenty or thirty of those green Army cots Tanzania had unloaded from out the jitney, and he was toting them one by one inside the house. Sweet heart of Jesus! Now I unloaded *myself* on this Kentucky Colonel. I asked him if he thinks I was born yesterday not to smell the caca stinking on my own doorstep – 'because if you thinks you'll turn this boarding house into a parlour for peddling *pussies* just like all the rest on this island you've got *another* thing coming –

95

because why the fuck does a pizza restaurant need *all* this amount of beds?'

The Colonel only smiled again and he said that come to think of it, he'd forgotten to mention about the cots, as in truth it seemed obvious enough to him. That if we were all going into business together, then the only appropriate place for him and he partner to reside was right here in the house with the rest of the soldiers. I told him straight away that Gregoria and me never agreed to *that* one as part of the deal – 'and in any case you and you partner are only *two* people – so why is that cabrón Tanzania toting inside the house enough Army cots to service an entire *regiment*?' But this Colonel only continued smiling, and he said it was obvious *he* was the first Kentucky Colonel ever to grace the presence of this boarding house – and I said yes, and I hope he's the last! – because a Kentucky Colonel could never bivouac anyplace a-tall without he troop of aids d'camp to attend him. *Ayeeyosmío!* I told this Colonel that not even the General *Eisenhower* required so many soldiers only to wipe he culo and sprinkle on some Johnsons powder and give it a few pats in the morning, and he and Tanzania could stay if they wanted and maybe a couple of those aids d'camp – but I was not allowing a single one of those Army cots inside the house – and if he didn't like it he could find someplace *else* to make he bivouac and he pizza parlour too!

So soon enough the boys arrived from the Base, and Tony started to slinging he pies, and in no time he had a dozen of those pizzas bubbling on top the table. Of course, not even a single customer had arrived yet to buy a pizza. But when we smelled those pies fresh out the oven like that, we couldn't *help* weself but eat a few slices each for we own dinner too, and Mrs Carmichael consumed an entire deluxe leaving behind only the circle of wet bread. There was still a half-dozen of those pies on the table when the Colonel started to packing them up in the pasteboard boxes, and he said he was going out in he motorcar to pick up a few deliveries. But I wanted to know who he thought he was delivering those pies to, as not a customer had called yet even with that telephone number blinking tall as the sky on top the roof? The Colonel only said again not to worry – that he had arranged everything with the boys at the Base, and they would all be here in full force tonight – and now he repeated heself even though we still didn't understand what the ass was the difference, that he was going out to *pick up* deliveries, not to drop them off.

So Gregoria and me and Mrs Carmichael and the boys sat waiting beneath this big empty Bailey and Barnum tent the whole night for not even a *customer* to arrive for a pizza. They all said of course that the best way to pass the time was for me to tell them a story and straight away Tony asked for the one of the man whose eggs were so big he had to carry them around in a shopping cart – and everybody started to shout and clap they hands, but I told them I was too depressed. It was near midnight when I announced at last that it was time for everybody to go to bed, but of course hardly were those words out my mouth when the Colonel pulled up in front the house with he Cadillac motorcar loaded to the whitewalls again with all those little boys – each one smiling with a slice of pizza chewing inside he mouth – and following behind was the *entire* American Army!

All in a sudden these jitneys and Jeeps full of American soldiers began to arrive, and in no time a-tall that tent big as a cricket oval was bursting open at the seams. Now all the soldiers began to beat they tin plates against the table for another pepperoni pie and more cerveza – each one with a little half-starved baboo sitting on he lap chewing a slice of pizza that was probably the first solid food he put in he mouth the whole week – and next thing you know Tony and the two boys could *never* hold theyselves back, and they were up on top the table again with they little white bamsees jiggling in the frilly pink panties! And as if all that was not *enough* scandal in the house for one night, when we turned around we saw up on top the table beside them, not *only* the old Syrian with he fat pumpulum jiggling just the same, but the little chuff-chuff Chief-of-Police with he special drawers in the red, white and blue stripes of the Union Jack too!

Sweet heart of Jesus! All in a sudden like these soldiers had all gone vie-kee-vie, and they started to bawl and whistle and beat they tin plates against the table for more pizza and more cerveza, and of course, just when you needed that Colonel and he pendejo Tanzania the most, they'd both flat disappeared. So Gregoria and me and Mrs Carmichael didn't have no choice now but to start making these pies *weselves* – even though we'd never attempted to sling a pizza in all we life – otherwise we would have had a *mutiny* on we hands of that portable mess filled the brim with drunken soldiers!

But after watching at Tony slinging pies for two days straight it didn't take us no time to catch on, and before you know we were all three spinning those pies up over we shoulders, down beneath we legs and back behind we backs, and Mrs Carmichael got so carried away that when she threw she pie up in the air it stuck to the roof of the tent. And Johnny, let me tell you we prepared *so* many of those pizza-pies that night – pepperoni and deluxe and anchovy and all the rest – that by the time we finished we could sling them with we eyes shut. By the time the very last one of those stone-drunk soldiers had picked heself up to stumble he way home – and he'd crawled out over the pile of dirty US Army tin plates, curls of pizza crust and tomato sauce and half-drunk bottles of cerveza mounted in a *moat* going right around the periphery of this big tent – by *that* time me and Gregoria and Mrs Carmichael were so exhausted we were ready to drop!

It was all we could manage to drag weselves upstairs and Mrs Carmichael down in she basement to sleep the sleep of the dead, so tired we couldn't even wake up the following morning to serve the soldiers they breakfast. *So* exhausted to we bones after this big palaver of the pizza parlour, that we slept straight through until three o'clock the following afternoon. Of course, by then I was so vex with that Kentucky Colonel and he partner Tanzania I was ready to string them both up by they stones – especially when I began to consider the wake of that destruction those drunken soldiers had left behind for Gregoria and me now to *clean up* – and this time I was determined to tell the Colonel and he devil Tanzania to pack up they portable mess and don't *never* come back!

But Johnny, when Gregoria and me took a deep breath, and we held hands together to brace weself, and we dared at last to go outside and survey the destruction that was the *whole* of that backyard only the previous night – we near pelted down in a heart attack again – because sure enough everything was clean, and tidy, and spotless like you could never even imagine! There was that Tanzania polishing with he shirttail the very last one of those stacks of *Property of the US Army* tin plates, all shining in the sun now like if they were Castleford china in truth! Beside him sitting on the bench was that Kentucky, and straight away he made a sign for Tanzania to take off running for the jitney, and he brought back a little metal strongbox with the Colonel's portrait painted on the top smiling just like he pasteboard barrels! Now he ordered Tanzania to open it up with a little key he had on a ring with all the rest hanging from he belt – and the Colonel began to take out all these packages of Yankee money, piling them up in two neat piles tall as those *same* stacks of tin plates! – and when Gregoria and me sat down he slid a pile over before each of us, reaching up high as we own narices. *Papa-yo!* Now the Colonel announced very proud that this was we portion of the take from those pies of last night – two-thousand-four-hundred-and-fifty American dollars each – and I whispered to Gregoria to let's take off running for that bank fast as we feet can carry us to hide it away, before this chupidee Colonel can realize he has made a miscount!

But the Colonel said not to worry about *that* – because one thing for sure he never made no mistakes in counting out money – and of course since we were all business partners we must go together to the bank and make we deposit, particular as Gregoria and me hadn't had an opportunity yet to ride in he Cadillac motorcar. 'But,' said this Kentucky Colonel, 'first it is only appropriate for all of us to drink a toast to the success of *Skippy's Pizza Parlour!*' And with that he sent Tanzania running to the jitney for five of those little shot glasses – because of course by now old Mrs Carmichael had ascended from she death downstairs in she catacombs too – and a bottle of special Kentucky bourbon called by the name of *Pavo Salvaje*. So the Colonel made a toast – and we all raised we glasses and knocked them together and fired them back – and then I made a toast, and Gregoria la Rosa and Mrs Carmichael and that Tanzania, and then we all made a toast again. Now I announced that we had better get weself going for the bank while there was still a chance to find it – much less the big Zeppelin-motorcar – and with that the Colonel took out he gold watch hanging on the chain from he vestcoat pocket, he snapped it open to check the time, and he said yes, now was the perfect moment to leave. So we all stood and me and Gregoria took up we stacks of money each one like a pile of schoolbooks tucked beneath we arms, and Johnny, straight away out from nowhere arrived that *same* little chuff-chuff Chief-of-Police from the previous night. He blew he whistle with he hand raised before him in a *halt!* like if he was directing traffic, he took out a big piece of rolled up paper from he pocket and snapped it open, and he presented us a summons of five-thousand dollars for

Operating a Restaurant Without a License

Sweet heart of Jesus! Now I could *never* hold myself back from letting loose on this little Chief-of-Police, and I told him he had every reason to inform us of this license last night before he started to carry on like that in the sacraledge of he Union Jack drawers – that he should not only be ashamed of heself and get a good cuttail, but courtmartialled too – and in any case five-thousand *coconut* dollars didn't mean nothing to us a-tall, not even a *fart!* Because of course, by now that Pavo Salvaje had gone a little bit to my head, and I told the Chief how soon enough we would all be *multi-multi-multi*-millionaires! How soon enough I would be the *Queen* of Pizzas over the entire Caribbean with Gregoria la Rosa my *Princess* in Waiting – and we would soon be using President *Franklins* to wipe we culos and light we cigars and not none of that coconut nastiness! – and with that I raised up my glass in the air for another toast.

But this chuff-chuff Chief-of-Police only continued smiling, and he informed us that according to the pact signed between we Royal Colonial Government and they own even before the first of those Yankee soldiers could set foot on this island, the only denomination we would accept from them was they *own* Yankee dollars. And since the Kentucky Colonel and he partner were both soldiers of the American Army, then this fine could only be paid in the real US dollars of we *own* cherished Uncle Sam – and not none of that 'coconut nastiness', as you rightly called them Mrs Domingo – and with that he raised up a glass in the air for a toast now *heself!* Johnny, we didn't have no choice but to hand it all over, even though we knew perfectly well this Chief-of-Police was only feeding us a boldface lie. Now he counted up all the money, and just as you have already realized we were a hundred dollars short, and he told us that if we didn't come up with the cash right now he wouldn't have no choice but to shut down we pizza parlour! Of course, we were all distressed by this and we didn't know what we would do, when next thing we saw Mrs Carmichael pulled out she *own* Franklin tucked between she tot-tots, and she said how it was a tip from one of those boys last night only to watch her try to eat a pepperoni sausage without a knife and fork. Now Mrs Carmichael raised up she glass in the air for another toast, and she said Skippy's Pizza Parlour was the best thing that happened to her since she husband pelted-off!

So the Chief-of-Police left with all we hard-earned money, and we all said what a terrible shame that he had robbed us boldface like that, and I raised my glass in the air and said, 'At least we still have we parlour!' So everybody fired one back, and then the Colonel made a toast, and Gregoria la Rosa and Tanzania and Mrs Carmichael, and when we finished that bottle of Pavo Salvaje we were still depressed, and the Colonel sent Tanzania running for another. Now I raised my glass and said, 'To the King of Fastfood of the entire world!' and the Colonel said yes, *that* is a fact. He said there ain't nobody knows the business better than him, and that was how he could assure us with perfect confidence that the thing we could *never* afford to do now was cry over we spilled milk. 'The thing with fastfood,' explained this colonel, 'is to strike back *aggressive*. To count up all the margins of we gains and losses, and take in for the full stock of the interest for we surplus value, plus the base price minus the dividends of all we bonus bogus expenditures' – or something so because of course *I* could never understand that language of fastfood – and he said the thing we must do now without even batting an eyelid, is to invest weself *twice* over! We must *double* up we commitment, and now the Colonel whispered for me to remind him again what was the precise figure that we had lost, since those little details sometimes slipped he mind – and I told him that it was five-thousand American dollars! – so he said in that case we must invest *ten*.

But I didn't have no experience with this kind of big business that everybody knows the Yankees are famous – that all I could know anything about was running the boarding house and raising cattle on the ranch in Venezuela ever since I was a little girl – but anyway just as always I couldn't *help* but put in my little two-cents. I said that if it was up to *me*, I wouldn't dig this financial pit any deeper than we had already dug it. Because in truth all we needed to put out for those pizzas tonight was a few cents for a sack of flour and a couple bottles of tomato catsup. Because after all those expenses of yesterday for that big Bailey and Barnum tent, and all the tables and benches and the buckets of knives and forks and that big roll of paper serviettes – not even mentioning only the *electricity* to keep that sign on top the roof blinking – did the Colonel really want to spend all this amount of money on top?

Now of course the Colonel started to whistling a different tune, and he said that in truth come to think of it he *was* a little bit out of he pockets after he recent expenditures, 'as all of you will presently see for youselves!' and with that he huffed and puffed a few times to go down on he knees in the dirt before me. *Well!* I was so startled by this peculiar exhibition all I could think was that the Colonel was going to dirty up the knees of he nice white pantaloons, when straight away he took from he vestcoat pocket a little black velvet box, and he announced in a loud voice for everybody to hear he proposal for the two of us to get weselves *hitched!* And Johnny, sure enough when I opened the little box there inside was the engagement ring glittering away, with the *biggest* diamond you have ever seen in all you life, big as you fist like this!

Johnny, when I saw this diamond glittering like that it made me vie-kee-vie first thing – because I said that in truth I'd married looks the last time, so maybe this time around I would settle for fortune and fame – and with that I tucked the little velvet box safe between my tot-tots. The Colonel let loose a bawl like if he was Johnny Weissmuller now swinging on a vine through the jungle, *Aye-ee-aye-ee-aye-ee-aye!* and he huffed and puffed a few more times to climb up and sit heself again on the bench beside me. Now of course he raised he glass in the air for a toast to the lady of the household – the most dignified, and exquisite, and beauteous woman on all the island – the Queen of Pizzas over the entire Caribbean:

Mrs Skippy Sanders!

So everybody knocked they glasses together and fired them back – everybody except *me* – because just as always when I was drinking I became a little bit more emotional than usual, and sensitive, and next thing you know big tears were rolling in a flood down my cheeks! The Colonel ripped me off a paper serviette very gallant from the big roll beside him, I patted my eyes a little bit and blew my nose, and I said that since I was going to be hitched soon I might as well make my confession and spill the truth. Because Johnny, the *other* thing about drinking alcohol is not only does it make me a little bit more emotional and sensitive than usual, and overgenerous, but bobo as a bubulups too!

Now I said that even though everybody thought I was only a poor destitute widow without a cent to she name, the truth was that Sergeant Warren had made me a present of ten-thousand Yankee dollars when we made the arrangements for this boarding house, that of course I had it hidden away safe in the bank. I said that of course neither the Colonel nor nobody else could know nothing about that money as it was top secret Army information – but since I was going to get hitched soon and rich and famous too – then that ten-thousand wasn't nothing more than a drop inside the bucket, so I might as well hand it over for the double-expansion of Skippy's Pizza! But before I could even have a chance to catch my breath after this long death-sentence I'd just pronounced, Gregoria came out with *we* top secret signal when one of us was in deep trouble, and she pointed she nose up in the air to sniff it a few times and say, 'I wonder what the fuck could be burning in the kitchen like that?' and two of us jumped up straight away. Of course, by this time I was so drunk that I fell straight down again *boodoops!* flat on top my face. But fortunate for me Gregoria took command of the situation, and she lifted me up off the ground to carry me in she arms all the way back inside the kitchen.

First thing she pelted me two hot slaps across my face, then she made me drink a strong coffee, and only when I could stand by myself without holding onto the wall, did she ask me if I'd lost my marbles in truth? Because how could I even *think* about handing over all that money to this Kentucky and he partner Tanzania – that anybody could take one look at them and know they were nothing more than a couple of crooks – and she couldn't believe she had such a foolish woman for she own *mummy!* Gregoria knew good enough that was the thing to make me feel worst of all and bring me back to my senses, and next thing you know I was blubbering like a baby again. Of course, Gregoria only pelted me two more hot slaps across my face, and now she asked me to please hand her over that diamond ring to take a look. So I fished it out from between my tot-tots, and of course, when Gregoria opened up the little black velvet box and she saw this diamond glittering away like that, now *she* was every bit as vie-kee-vie as I was only a moment before – but at least she was a little bit more practical – because she said the thing we had to do was to find some way to 'out-crook the crooks', and get this diamond ring away from that Colonel 'without the hitching part'. Because just as Gregoria rightly said, not even the entire Crown Jewels of Queen Elizabeth *sheself* was compensation enough for waking up in the morning beside that chuff-chuff little Colonel, not to mention having to call him *daddy!*

So two of us considered for a moment the consequences of this predicament and what we would do. I said maybe the best strategy was to pay out that money for the expansion of Skippy's Pizza, because sure enough in two or three nights we would make it straight back again without a problem – but I would tell the Colonel I was hanging on to that ring as a *lagniappe* – just so he understood perfectly well there ain't no hitching thrown in in the bargain. Of course, Gregoria was always a step ahead of me when it came to business, and she said the thing to do was to settle not *only* for that ring as a lagniappe – because who knows it might even be a fake? – but to make the Colonel hand over half the shares of he Kentucky restaurant there beside the Base *too*, everything fifty-fifty, because she didn't care if she ate another slice of pizza in all she life! I told Gregoria she had a brilliant mind when it came to business – that if Columbus would have met *her* on the dock instead of she grandparents *we* would own the whole of Europe by now and America too, instead of the other way around – and that was just the deal that I would strike up with the Colonel! My ten-thousand for half he Kentucky Fried restaurant and half the pizza parlour *plus* the diamond ring as a lagniappe – but there ain't no hitching fringe benefits thrown in in this deal a-tall! – and when I told the Colonel he let loose another bawl like Johnny Weissmuller swinging on the vine again. So now we all went to load weself up in he big Cadillac to go to the bank, but I told him to hand over those keys because *I* was driving – so let's see what kind of speed this Zeppelin-motorcar could do – and first stop is *Kentucky Fried* to pick up a barrel!

Johnny, we couldn't help weself but pick up two more barrels on the way back home from the bank to have for we dinner, and the Colonel and Tanzania dropped us off and they left with the ten-thousand in cash for the double-expansion of Skippy's Pizza. Of course, the soldiers and Gregoria and me and Mrs Carmichael had already devoured those two barrels down to they final drumstick, and we were waiting there beneath the big empty tent until almost midnight, before the Colonel could pull up at last with he motorcar loaded to the whitewalls again with all he little boys. Following in he wake of course was Tanzania in the big camouflaged jitney, with that same cavalcade of the American forces blowing they horns behind them too! Of course, by this time I was spitting fire again I was so vex, and I asked the Colonel how the fuck he expected to get time to assemble the second big Bailey and Barnum tent, and the second set of tables and benches and eating utensils and all the rest for the double-expansion of the pizza parlour, because those soldiers were ready right *now* to lead they assault on us for all they pies and cerveza?

But the Colonel only smiled as usual and he told me not to worry, that he had Tanzania already busy unloading the 'replicate facilities for the double-amplification of Skippy's Pizza to the tune of ten-thousand clams' – because of course he had to bamboozle me with some more of he fastfood-talk – and now he took us around the house to see Tanzania straining and sweating away to make all the preparations. But Johnny, when I peered in the back of that jitney and my eyes grew accustomed to the dark – and I saw just *how* this Tanzania was straining heself – I dropped *boo-doops!* to the ground again, this time

in a dead faint. Because all Tanzania had in the back of that jitney was another one of those rusty old good-for-nothing
Dutch ovens the two of them had purchased someplace, not
even worth *ten cents!* After they woke me up with a bucket of
icewater they had to carry me and put me to sit beneath the
tent, and they gave me a shot of Pavo Salvaje to settle my
nerves. And Johnny, when I came to my senses again and I
realized that this terrible nightmare was *real* – that that
chupidee Colonel had in fact thrown away my ten-thousand
Yankee dollars on another worthless old rusty up Dutch oven
– I couldn't help myself from firing a next shot of Pavo Salvaje,
and a next, and I didn't slow down until my face was flat on the
table in one of those same *Property of the US Army* tin plates, out
cold unconscious for the third time today!

This time I woke up to discover myself stark naked in some
bed that didn't even *belong* to me! There beside me stark naked
too was a white walrus I couldn't even *identify* – and I was
ready to let loose a bawl to wake the dead – before I realized of
course that he was none other than the Kentucky Colonel. Now
I realized that this was he *own* bed where he'd performed on
me who knew *what* amount of nasty perversions the whole
night long, with me there passed out cold unconscious from all
that Pavo Salvaje. Sweet heart of Jesus! Straight away I broke
down weeping again – and I checked my finger quick to see
that I was still wearing the diamond engagement ring –
because my sole consolation in all my state of disgrace was that
at least this cabrón Kentucky had pledged heself to marry me
before the altar! Of course, he was there beside me only snort-
ing away like the fat walrus suffering from a case of whoopingcough – and when I examined him close I wasn't even sure
I didn't *prefer* my state of eternal disgrace than to waking up

every morning for the rest of my days beside *him* – just as my beloved Gregoria had foretold! Now I jumped up from out the bed and I wrapped the sheet around me, because I had to find her straight away, as Gregoria was the only person in the world to take me in she arms and console me and advise me what to do. But Johnny, when I opened the door and stuck my head in the hallway I was near *decapitated* by a half-naked soldier chasing a baby baboo – and he was waving a Franklin in the air behind him calling *cutchie-cutchie-cutchie!* – that I was so *scandalized* by this thing going on in my own house, I could only slam the door back again and pretend I never saw it! After a moment I cracked it open again and fortunate for me they'd both disappeared, so I took off in a bolt with the sheet around me down the corridor to Gregoria's bedroom.

I knocked on the door very soft, and I waited a moment before I opened it quiet to let myself in. But Johnny, *when* I looked inside that room to see what was taking place, my eyeballs near jumped out they sockets! Instead of Gregoria sleeping peaceful like I was expecting, there was an orgy of bullers going on with five or six of those American soldiers in the bed – and some more on top the bureau, down on the ground and posted up against the wall – and each soldier had for he partner one of those poor helpless half-starved little baboos. Sweet heart of Jesus! One by one I checked every last bedroom, and in every last one it was the same orgy going on in full swing, and now I was *desperate* to find Gregoria but she wasn't nowhere in the house! I was sitting there on the floor at the end of one of those corridors with the bedsheet still wrapped around me, still weeping, when all in a sudden I thought of something. And Johnny, I wasn't liking this thing *a-tall!* Now I jumped up again to hurry down the corridor and knock on the door just beside the Colonel's own – which of course was the only one I'd forgotten to check as it was the adjoining bedroom of that

Tanzanian Devil – and of course, who should answer but my own beloved Gregoria la Rosa! She was standing there before me stark naked with the sheet wrapped around her, the two of us *not* like mother and daughter now, but looking instead like identical twins. Only *one* twin was weeping hysterical drowning in she nightmare of *hell* that had descended on her so sudden to invade she own home – and the *other* was smiling calm and peaceful and bobo as a bubulups like she'd just ascended into heaven!

Of course, there in the bed behind her was that Tanzania snoring away, and when I realized what *she* had been doing while that wadjank Kentucky had me captive dishonouring me the whole night long, I got so vex I pelted her two hot slaps across she face! Of course, Gregoria only continued smiling like the little girl with the spider tickling inside she panties, and she took me in she arms regardless of those slaps to offer me consolation, and she whispered, 'OK Mummy, tell me what is wrong!' By now of course I was weeping hysterical and I couldn't even catch my breath to answer, and Gregoria had to hug me tight a few minutes and dry my tears with the corner of the sheet, before I could explain to her how that pendejo Kentucky had practised every kind of wicked perversion on me all night long with me passed out cold from all that Pavo Salvaje – that my sole consolation in the world was that I couldn't remember a thing! – but at least that Colonel had pledged heself to marry me before the altar. Gregoria only continued smiling – until she began to laugh out loud! – that I became so vex again with her for making a joke like this out of my dreadful predicament, I couldn't help but pelt her two more slaps across she face.

Gregoria continued laughing even still – and when at last *she* could recover sheself and catch she breath – she told me that unlike he partner there snoring away after *she* had exercised him the whole night long so wonderful to shake the earth, didn't I realize that that Kentucky Colonel was the biggest *buller* in the entire American Army! Now Gregoria explained how it was she who carried me upstairs *sheself*, and she undressed me and put me to sleep after I'd passed out borracho like that – but of course she had no choice but to put me in the Colonel's bed as it was the only one empty in the whole house – and furthermore, since that Colonel was such a buller, it was the *safest* place for her to leave me too. Johnny, I was so happy to hear this news that I kissed Gregoria on both cheeks and hugged her tight again, and I told her the only thing to do now was to figure out some way to get rid of that Kentucky and he partner this time for *good*. Gregoria said yes, now that she had taken Tanzania for all the pleasure he was worth she was ready to send him packing – and furthermore she'd already taken care of that one too without a worry – and now she raised up she left hand to show me a *next* engagement ring with a *next* maco diamond big as you fist like this glittering away! But Johnny, I was all confused again and I asked Gregoria what the fuck she was talking about, because now I was stuck not *only* with that Kentucky Colonel as my husband for the rest of we lives without escape, I was stuck with that Tanzania for my own son-in-law too!

Gregoria only continued smiling and she told me that first of all, didn't I realize those diamonds were fake as a couple chips of coca-cola glass-bottle? And second, didn't I know the quickest way to scare off a couple of scoundrels like those two was to get them to promise to carry us before the altar? Because one thing she could *guarantee* good as gold, was that soon as these two woke up tomorrow morning to realize the predicament *we'd* gotten them into now, they would take off running first thing with they tails hanging limp between they legs! And now Gregoria told me the best way to make *sure*, was to carry myself *straight* back to bed beside my white walrus! So what to do, Johnny? I could only trust Gregoria and hope she knew what the ass she was talking about – and in any case I was too confused now by all this commess to decide for myself! – so I took her in my arms one last moment before I turned to drag myself down the corridor back to the Colonel's bed. And Johnny, the truth is that by this time I was so exhausted, I dropped straight asleep even despite that walrus with he whoopingcough snoring in the bed beside me.

So exhausted to my bones that I slept straight through until three o'clock the following afternoon. Sure enough just as Gregoria had foretold there wasn't no white walrus with he whoopingcough in the bed beside me, and when I got up to peer through the window and spy in the backyard, sure enough there wasn't no big Bailey and Barnum tent neither. No benches, nor tables, nor even the banner blowing in the breeze like the best of all possible titles for this story of we *Portable Mess*, no *nothing* remaining of that Kentucky Colonel and he Tanzanian Devil a-tall! I could only stand there at the window smiling ear-to-ear, and listen for a moment to that sound of perfect silence in the house for the first time in a week since those two scamps arrived to turn the world upside-down. But then all in a sudden it dawned upon me like a bombshell what they had disappeared *with*, and I wrapped the sheet around me to take off running down the corridor, back to Tanzania's bedroom.

Of course, Gregoria was still sleeping like if she was dead after all she exercise and excitement all night long the previous night, and by the time I shook her awake I was already blubbering like a baby again. Gregoria could only take me in she arms to offer me consolation and whisper, 'OK Mummy, tell me what is wrong *now!*' and when I caught my breath I said didn't she realize that those two scoundrels had taken off with my ten-thousand Yankee dollars! But Gregoria only continued to hug me and console me, still smiling ear-to-ear like she pussy was *imprinted* with the memory of that Tanzania in all he proportions and she couldn't forget it a-tall – that now I was starting to get vex again ready to pelt her some more hot slaps – when straight away she reached she hand beneath the bed to take out the little metal strongbox. Of course, painted on top just the same as those pasteboard barrels was the portrait of that Kentucky Colonel, and when Gregoria opened it up with the little key hanging with she crucifix now on the chain around she *own* neck, it was full to the brim overflowing with nothing less than *Franklins!* Johnny, I didn't have no idea how Gregoria could have possibly tempted, or tantalized, or thiefed this strongbox away from that Tanzania – and I didn't even care to find out for myself – because when I caught a whiff of all the money green like that it sent me vie-kee-vie first thing, and all I wanted to do was to count it out! I dumped it right there in the middle of the bed, and we spread it across the sheet in *twenty* stacks of *ten* Franklins in each stack, or *twenty*-thousand Yankee dollars. *Oui fute, pupu-yo!* I could only let loose a cry of joy and I told Gregoria to let's throw on some clothes and take off running for the bank. Of course, we couldn't even reach the front gate before that same pendejo chuff-chuff of a Chief-of-Police appeared out from nowhere. He blew he whistle with he hand out before him in a halt like if he was directing traffic again, he took the big piece of rolled up paper from he pocket and snapped it open, and he presented us with a summons of twenty-thousand this time for

Prostitution and They Illegal Trafficking

Sweet heart of Jesus! I couldn't help but unload myself again on this little Chief-of-Police, and I asked him what the fuck he was talking about that this was a respectable boarding house of Uncle Sam and I didn't permit no prostitutes to come in here a-tall, and furthermore, the only three women to pass though these doors in over a *week* now since the Colonel invaded with all he troops of bullers was Gregoria, and me, and poor old Mrs Carmichael! But he only continued smiling just as always, and he said how first of all, *that* was just who he was talking about. You, and Gregoria, and poor old feeble Mrs Carmichael – or should we call she by she professional name of *Penelope Pepperoni?* – because please tell me in which bed each of *you* spent the night last night? Johnny, I was ready to take out my pearl-handled pistol and fight him a duel right there in front the house for insulting the honour of the three of us like that, when he said that in any case it was the *second* charge of this summons that was the incriminating one. He said that what he was referring to specifically was all those little boys at a hundred dollars each for those American soldiers, in addition to the *free deliveries* from the big white Cadillac motorcar of that Kentucky Colonel going on all night up and down to every boarding house between here and Point Cumana!

So what to do, Johnny? Because even though I didn't know nothing about no deliveries, I knew good enough that everything he said about the goings-ons of those poor little boys and the soldiers last night was true enough, as I had been in every one of those bedrooms and seen for myself. Still, I knew just as well how that buller of a Chief-of-Police had been in a good number of those rooms *heself*, and not only to write out he police-report! Now he took away the strongbox from me and the little key from Gregoria hanging around she neck – he counted it all out and of course there wasn't a single Franklin remaining inside when he handed the box back to me with a big smile on he face to match the portrait of the *other* pendejo – and that was that!

Johnny, there wasn't nothing we could do. Just turn around

114

again and go back inside the house and start to prepare a big jorum of mondongo that the soldiers could take for they dinner, because of course they would be home from the Base in a few minutes. So I put the empty strongbox with the picture of that Kentucky on the shelf beside the jar of sugarcakes to remember we adventure by, and when the boys arrived they all said how they should have *never* allowed me to get involved with that Colonel. How everybody on the Base knew he was nothing but a scoundrel, and a thief, and what a shame that due to him I had lost all that amount of money! But I told them it wasn't the money that had me feeling bad. Not ten-thousand, nor twenty, nor even a million – because I have never been a millionaire in my life and I don't want to be a millionaire – what had me feeling *worst* of all was all those abuses to the poor little boys. And now I reprimanded my soldiers to tell them that furthermore, I hope *they'd* confined they *own* scandal to that burlesque dance up on top the tables, and they hadn't involved theyselves in none of that wickedness going on in the bedrooms *upstairs*. Of course, they didn't say too much more for the remainder of dinner. And when we finished we soursop icecream for dessert, and it was time for me to give them a story, I said that I wouldn't be able to tonight because I wanted them to help me return that old Dutch oven back to the Syrian, as in truth, I'd felt bad ever since we thiefed it boldface like that. I told them how we had the other oven anyway that the Colonel purchased if we ever wanted to make a pie for weself – but this story had left such a bad taste in my mouth for pizza, that it wouldn't be for a good long while – so let's just return the Syrian's old oven to finish this story one time and call it at last *The End*.

But Johnny, this story was not yet finished as you might have guessed. Because when Gregoria and me and Mrs Carmichael loaded up the oven with the soldiers in the back of the Jeep, and we pulled into the drive at Mucurapo, what did we find parked outside but the big white Cadillac, and right there beside it was the camouflaged jitney too! So almost before we could have a chance to dump that rusty old oven in the backyard, Mrs Carmichael was there behind the bush peering in through the window, and two seconds later we were all there beside her. Of course, who should we find sitting in the Syrian's livingroom besides heself, and the Colonel, and he partner Tanzania, but that *same* chuff-chuff of a Chief-of-Police too. They were all four of them there toasting they successes each with a little glass in he hand, and a bottle of Pavo Salvaje, and just there beside it on the coffeetable in four neat piles was all the money!

Of course, the strategy for this invasion was so obvious there wasn't any need for me to even explain. Just to hand out the various assignments, and tell Tony how he would be the first to enter and sabotage them on the coffeetable with he little white bamsee and he frilly pink panties, but it was *he* objective to detain the old Syrian in the master bedroom. Next to sustain the assault would be the second soldier with the second round of he own little white bamsee and frilly pink panties, and he would torpedo the Chief-of-Police in the bedroom beside the parlour. Then to continue the attack would be the third soldier, and he mission was to crabhole Kentucky in the bedroom at the back. Last, of course, to lead us on to victory in the kitchen would be Gregoria la Rosa, and she would kamikaze that Tanzanian Devil with the *secret weapon* – and with that I reached between my tot-tots and of course everybody was expecting me to remove my pearlhandled pistol – but what I took out instead was something much more lethal: a tiny tin of little anchovy fish.

Johnny, this plan worked just as beautiful as you could imagine. In no time a-tall they were all four of them immobilized in the separate quarters of the house, and me and old Mrs Carmichael entered to confiscate all the money – pausing only long enough to toast we success with a shot of Pavo Salvaje – before we could take off with the siren braying *he-haw he-haw he-haw* like the donkey with laryngitis again, as fast as that Jeep could carry us straight to the bank!

So Johnny, now at last we have reached we happy ending. Because Gregoria and Tony and the two soldiers and especially Mrs Carmichael were happy they'd had they adventure, with that metal strongbox with the portrait of Kentucky smiling chupidee between the jar of saltprunes and the jar of sugarcakes on the counter to remind them too. I was happy of course to have my story and my ten-thousand dollars back again, and it was that money that went to sustain you uncles studying medicine in Canada, and all the rest of us here just the same. But most important of everybody were those half-starved little baboos, and cocoa-pañols, and negritos, since *they* ended up happy too. Because of course, of that twenty-thousand me and Gregoria deposited in the bank, ten belonged to *them*. The only thing was we couldn't just hand them over all that amount of money, as they would never learn the lesson of right and wrong nor how to behave theyselves proper like that. It was Gregoria sheself who thought up the plan what to do. To go together that same evening to the American Base, and to tell this entire story from beginning to end no matter *how* tedious and how painful, to my old friend the Sergeant Warren.

Of course, Sergeant Warren could never *believe* a story so far-fetched as this one. So to prove it we jumped in the Jeep and took him straight away to the little house on Mucurapo Road, and sure enough parked in front still were not only the big white Cadillac, but that camouflaged jitney of the US Army with the whole of that *Portable Mess* packed up inside it too. And as soon as they saw the face of Sergeant Warren at the front door, that Kentucky Colonel and he devil Tanzania took off running out the *back* – they jumped in they Cadillac motorcar with the tires smoking and they didn't slow down before they reached as far as Australia – because it was a long time before anybody heard word of those two again. As for the Chief-of-Police and the old Syrian, there wasn't no place for them to run a-tall. In two seconds Sergeant Warren had them both under military arrest for possession of that stolen US Army jitney and all its contents. But the Sergeant told them both that he was prepared to forget the whole thing, but only on *two* conditions. First, the old Syrian must convert he house into a boarding home for underprivileged boys. Second, the Chief-of-Police must dedicate heself to training and preparing these boys for a profession in the police forces when they grow up.

And so it happened that those ten-thousand dollars that belonged to the boys went for the *triple*-expansion of that little house into a boarding home *bigger* than the one that I had on Rust Street for the soldiers. And the next time you go to Mucurapo you can see it for youself, complete with the big sign on top the roof that reads

Skippy's Boarding Home for Underprivileged Boys

and of course, that was just how the police forces of this island came to be inundated mostly by bullers to this very day. So those little boys ended up happy just like the rest of us. We were all *especially* happy on Thursday nights – because every Thursday night in Mucurapo was *pizza*-night – with me and Gregoria and old Mrs Carmichael going to visit the boys, and the Chief-of-Police and the old Syrian. So every Thursday night it was the three of us slinging all those pies behind we backs, down beneath we legs and up over we shoulders, and we baked them until they were cripsy and bubbling in that Dutch oven too. And for a good many of those Thursday evenings Tony and the two soldiers would accompany us on pizza-nights to offer the boys a little entertainment. With all of us shouting, and clapping we hands together, and laughing till we had tears in we eyes, because those were some of the few good memories remaining with us from that long-ago time of the war.

4

The Tale of How Iguana Got Her Wrinkles
or The True Tale of El Dorado

for Janine Antoni

Ayeeyosmío! You want me to give you this nasty story? Well
you best push up close here beside me so I don't have to talk
too loud. Even though at ninety-six years of age I can't make so
much more noise anyway, and worse still since I lost the teeth.
Because when the man carried them the other day with me
bawling *thief! thief!* behind him, he only continued climbing
through the window smiling he big horsesmile at me with my
own teeth in he mouth, and me there with my gums and my
lips flapping, and nothing more than the soft *thufft! thufft!* like
a fart coming out my mouth. Sweet heart of Jesus! So I don't
have my jewels no more – that is how I used to call the teeth –
and when I try to talk up loud everything comes out in a jum-
ble beneath the shower, but Johnny, it would take *plenty* more
than that to shut me up. And we got to be careful just the same,
even if we don't talk no louder than a whisper. Because if you
mummy only hears me telling you this nasty story – particular
when I reach to the main part that concerns, of course, the *pussy*
of this younggirl – she will put us both out the house before we
can catch we breath. That is one word to grate up against she
ears in truth, that every time I am giving a joke or telling a story
and I forget myself and let it escape, you poor mummy gets
that look on she face red red like she's trying to make a caca
with a corcho inside she culo! You daddy too, never mind
when he was a youngboy this one was he favorite of all my stories. You daddy, and he wicked brothers, and all they badjohn-

120

boyfriends begging me again and again please to give them the story of the old iguana – even though it was the younggirl's *pussy* they wanted to hear about, and not that old wrinkled up iguana a-tall – because of course, there ain't nothing in the world to excite the blood of the youngboys more than *that*.

Well then, it happened in the old old time, this story. Back in the very beginning, when the first of those explorers from Spain and England arrived in this Caribbean, and the only people they found here living happy and peaceful enough were Amerindians, Caribs and Arawacks and Warrahoons and such. The explorers came, as you know youself, searching out the famous El Dorado, Sir Walter Raleigh leading the English, and Fernando de Berrío the Spanish. Sir Walter was the tall, handsome Captain dressed fancy in he jacket of red velvet, and he pantaloons, he white shirt with the collar of ruffles shoved up against he chin. Always reciting he love poetry, even at the moment of he brutal attacks. And de Berrío was the short, funny-looking fellow with he little round paunch – he tin costume creaking from the caballeros of the century before – with he little legs shaped in a bow from all those years riding on a horse. Always disappearing down in he cabin in the middle of he fierce battles, plagued either by seasickness, or he frequent diarrhoea. So those were the two who came with they fleets of ships, and of course it was we misfortune to get Fernando de Berrío, the Captain from Spain, because he was the one who decided that this El Dorado they were both looking for so crazy, was hidden somewhere right here on this island of Corpus Christi. Sir Walter made up he mind it was somewhere else – up the river Orinoco in what we now call Venezuela – or hidden somewhere along the coast of what we now know as Guyana.

But Johnny, the truth is that these two spent as much time watching each *other*, as they did searching out the gold. Each was afraid the other would find it first, so every time they heard a rumour or got a premonition that the other one was close, they would go straight away and ransack him. This would mean he would have to recover heself – and repair he ships and send to England or Spain for more soldiers so he could start he expedition all over again – but of course, before he could begin again he had to retaliate and attack the other. Back and forth and back and forth so many times that it's not surprising they never *did* find the gold, even after all those years, even if there was any gold to find here a-tall. Johnny, the truth is that all this El Dorado business wasn't nothing more than the fantasy of everybody's imagination. Growing bigger and bigger all the time, otherwise it could never have sent them so vie-kee-vie as it did.

Because not only didn't they know where was this El Dorado, they didn't know *what* it was neither. Some said how it was the long lost city of those Chibchas – another of the ancient Amerindian tribes – with the houses and the furnitures made solid from silver, all adorned in diamonds, and rubies, and every kind of jewel that you could name, and the streets paved only in gold. Some said how it was the mausoleum of a great Arawack king, or the emperor of those Incas from Peru, hidden high in the mountains. Others said that it was not the creation of a man, but some marvel of the earth itself. A river in the forest overflowing with water that was molten gold, or a lake, or the famous fountain of youth. And if you bathed youself in that golden water it could cure all you diseases – particular syphilis and the rest of that nastiness they brought with them from Europe that had they toe-tees turning green, and rotting off, and all those poor Amerindians dropping down like flies – that fountain of youth that could cure all you diseases, and you could live happy forever. Others said that it was a secret fruit, or flower, and if you ate some you shit would come out in shining bars. Others said how this fruit was the very same one out the

Bible, and when you ate it the bar would appear instant in *front* – blossoming out to burst open you zipper – tall and permanent like a golden obelisk almost to touch you nose. And Johnny, with that standpipe standing up like that and all those beautiful Amerindian slavegirls, you could live happy forever too! They just didn't know. And the more they talked about it and ransacked each other the more excited they became, and the more frustrated, until after a time they'd work theyselves up into a *frenzy* to find this El Dorado. Only beating the Indians and torturing them and dragging them from one place to the next to show them the secret, or tell them in a language they couldn't even understand – wherever or whatever it was – with the poor Indians the most confuffled of all.

So it was this same Fernando de Berrío, as I was saying, who arrived here in Corpus Christi with he fleet of ships, and he built the first houses – the jail and the church and the palace for the governor – the first settlement of Europeans here on the island. They were mostly Spanish. But some of them were also French, Portugee and Italian and whoever else wanted to come – anybody but *English* – and the name of this settlement was *Demerara*. The very same settlement that years later came to be called St Mary, and still later St Maggy. But it was named Demerara first for the crystals of sugar they would send back on the ships to Europe. That way the ships could return loaded with salted hams, Spanish wine and French champagne, Edam cheeses from Holland like cannonballs in they skins of red wax, clothes and books and guns and whatever else they needed. After a time, though, they began to say how those same yellow-brown crystals of Demerara sugar was the very El Dorado they were looking for, because after they sold it off, those ships were returning to Corpus Christi loaded down mostly with gold. But Johnny, the true El Dorado in all that sugar commerce wasn't those demerara crystals a-tall. It was the same yellow-brown *Amerindians* the Europeans put as slaves to clear the ground and grow the cane and make the sugar, and they beat them so much and worked them so hard, they were killing them off as quick as they could make they-selves a fortune.

Of course, the main reason for all that sugar was to finance the explorations of Fernando de Berrío. But before he could leave de Berrío had to put somebody in charge of Demerara. For this reason he sent to Spain for he partner in the sugar trad-ings, Don Antonio Sedeño, to pick up heself and come to Cor-pus Christi straight away. De Berrío wrote a letter at the same time to the King of Spain – because of course at this time Cor-pus Christi and all these islands belonged to the Spanish crown – that the King could name Don Antonio the first governor of the island. So it happened, and if you look in you history book you will see how it is true, that Don Antonio Sedeño was the first governor of Corpus Christi.

So now at last de Berrío could gather up he soldiers and he ships and leave on he first expedition. Because they had to make those expeditions by sea and not by land – an unfortu-nate thing for de Berrío, considering especially he seasickness and persistent ricewater-stools – as that jungle was too thick and dangerous with poisonous snakes for them to penetrate. That first expedition de Berrío intended to study the pitchlake at La Brea in the south of the island, and search the length of the coast beside it. Because de Berrío had read long before in the logs of Columbus how he went there to collect tar to stop-up holes in the bottoms of he ships. And Columbus wrote how that pitchlake was a marvel of nature that nobody never saw nothing like it before, 'not even the dancing troubadour-don-key from Seville!' so maybe the earth could have made the natural marvel of that *golden* lake somewhere beside it too?

But no sooner did de Berrío raise he sails when Sir Walter Raleigh, as was he habit, came straight away to ransack Demerara and burn the Church of San José de Irura flat to the ground. At the same time Sir Walter rescued those five little Amerindian kings de Berrío had chained together in the jail. Wannawanari, Tanoopanami, Maquarami, Atrimi and Caroni – that the hardest thing for me about telling this story is trying to pronounce those names – the five of them standing there naked, and trembling, they backsides pressed curious against the wall. Until Sir Walter turned them each slowly around, and he discovered they bamsees singed from the torture of those burning pokers and boiling pigfat.

That was the year of 1595. So de Berrío had to change he course and come straight back before he could begin he explorations, and he had to build back everything that Raleigh destroyed. But this time he built a big wall going right around Demerara, and the big fortress up above the harbour shooting off plenty cannons, and this time too, when he set sail on he expedition at last, he left half he soldiers there with Don Antonio. Of course, before he could begin he expedition again he had to sail all the way up the river Orinoco. Because first he was obliged to ransack Raleigh and take back he five little Amerindian kings, each dressed up now in they *own* frilly white shirt with the sleeves reaching down past they knees, a pair of red velvet pantaloons dragging around they ankles.

And now at last Don Antonio could send to Spain for he wife and he two daughters, because he had to leave them behind when he came running to Corpus Christi in such a hurry. He wife was a very stern and pious woman. *So* pious she used to shave she head bald like a nun, and she pledged sheself to dress only in black – this was the sign that she was mourning the death of she husband in advance – and she name was *Doña*

María Penitencia. With the two daughters called *María Dolores* and *María Consuelo*. Three Marías, and just as you would expect from names like these, the three of them were only for the Church. María Dolores and María Consuelo were the two doting acolytes of the old Archbishop, assisting him to prepare the altar and light the incense and fill the silver bowl with communion breads for all the Masses. Attending him the whole day long to put on and take off and put on again all he vestments. Because in addition to he several complete outfits for each of the Masses, he had another special green costume only to walk the garden, and a white one only for he midday meditation – a yellow one to greet the sick and a red one for the poor – and another complete *brown* costume with hat and cape and tall leather cowboy boots, only to stoop behind the bush when he received the calling. With the mother, María Penitencia she-self, sewing out with she own hand he long robe of purple silk for him to hear the penance, forty-two mother-of-pearl buttons going from beneath he chin all the way down to he toes! And, of course, those three Marías could *never* come to this place of heathens in the savage Caribbean, without bringing with them they old Archbishop.

They arrived to find Don Antonio still fast asleep for he afternoon siesta, and when they tiptoed quiet inside to lift the sheet and take a peek, there sleeping beside him in all she natural beauty, naked as the day she was born, was he little Amerindian slavegirl. So the first job for this Archbishop now that he had reached the New World – soon as they could bring he big trunk from off the ship – was to dress heself in he special costume for excising Caribbean devils, and pray over the head of Don Antonio. Now the two Marías could assist him to change he outfit to the one of purple silk, and they gave him a chalice of

126

wine to satisfy he thirst. Now the Archbishop could take from out he trunk the instrument they called the 'cat-of-the-nine-tales', and he delivered one hundred hot lashes to the little slavegirl. Poor child could scarce stand by the time he finished. But now at least María Penitencia was satisfied enough, ready to let loose the child that she could return to she family in the forest. Because in truth this little slavegirl was a princess very precious to she own Arawack people – the daughter of that same Wannawanari King that de Berrío had locked up in the jail – with she royal family waiting anxious for her on the other side of the island.

They *would* have let her return home to she royal family too, if it wasn't for one thing already obvious for all of them to see, that this little slavegirl was pregnant with the child of Don Antonio. So they couldn't send her home straight away. Instead, they locked her up in the cell downstairs in the base-ment, with María Dolores and María Consuelo bringing her she food every morning, nothing but a piece of Johnny cake and a glass of coconut water. But Don Antonio had a kind heart, and late each night he would tiptoe down the stairs to bring the child something proper to eat. Of course, most nights Don Antonio would get carried away with heself, and the two Marías would discover him early the next morning still consol-ing he little slavegirl, there struggling beneath him in she ham-mock tied in the corner.

The baby was born premature. A tiny creature with trans-parent skin and all the branches of blue veins showing, shiny red eyes like those of a salamander, and it didn't have no eye-brows nor lashes nor nails at the ends of its fingers and toes, only tiny cups like the suckers of a frog. But this little slavegirl loved she baby just the same. Cooing and talking to it soft and gentle in the language none of them could understand, and she wouldn't let she little salamander out from she hands for even a second. In truth, she would have remained happy enough locked up there in she cell for the rest of she days, before she lost that child. But they took it away from her just the same. And they called in two big soldiers to knock her down and beat her and bind she hands and feet, and they carried her off still struggling inside the banana peel of she little hammock, back to she family in the forest.

It was those two Marías who raised up this child, because every time they gave it to they mother to hold, María Penitencia, she only wanted to pelt it out the window. The Marías used to keep it in a shoebox in the corner of they room, some dry grass sprinkled at the bottom. And they tried to feed it every kind of fly and mosquito and spider that they could find – until they discovered the only *one* thing this little salamander liked to eat – and that was the green green dasheen leaves growing beneath a full moon beside the river, soft and wet with dew. So very early every morning the two Marías would get up faithful to go and collect them. It was a little girl, and the Marías called her by the same name as she mummy, *Iwana*, which in the language of the Arawacks means 'iguana'. And when she began to crawl the two Marías would carry her out in the yard every afternoon, each taking they turn to walk behind her, attached to a long string tied around she neck. Until one afternoon when Iwana got loose and took off running up the tall poinciana tree, she legs and arms turning at she sides like the blades of an airplane – which is just the way iguanas run if you've ever see them – and she remained up in that tree for three days. Until the two Marías attended the old Archbishop to dress in he green costume for walking the garden, and he climbed up in the poinciana heself to bring her down.

The Marías continued to feed her the soft dasheen leaves every day, and Iwana continued to grow, that after a time nobody didn't take hardly no notice of her inside the house.

Scrambling between they legs each time they came through the door, and climbing up to sit draped like a scarf around they necks, or curled comfortable in they laps every evening beneath the dinner table. Sometimes they would realize all in a sudden that nobody had seen little Iwana the whole week – with everybody taking off crazy to search in all the drawers, and the cupboards, and beneath the beds – because they were all afraid María Penitencia would stumble across her first. Like the time Iwana crawled down in the drain of the kitchen sink, and María Penitencia opened the pipe full and almost drowned her.

But in time even *she* seemed to grow accustomed to Iwana's presence in the house. Before they could turn around she'd grown up into a little girl, and just as you would expect from a tale like this – despite that Iwana was born such an ugly baby – she grew into the most *beautiful* younggirl Demerara had ever seen. Because don't forget that this Iwana, like she mummy before her, was a princess of royal Arawack blood. In addition to being the very first child of the New World to come out half-Spanish and half-Amerindian, and as always happens with mixtures like that, she took the best features from both. Tall and slim with golden skin and green almond eyes, she long dark hair reaching all the way down she back. And Johnny, every bit as beautiful as this child's looks were she gentle ways, calm and quiet and so graceful – that every time she passed you in the street hurrying back and forth between the governor's palace and that church – you couldn't help but feel a pang of pity. Because just as you would suppose too from a tale like this, the more beautiful and kind was this Iwana, the more cruel those two Marías treated her, and they mother, María Penitencia.

They put her to clean the palace and cook the food and wash all the clothes, not only those of the household, but now Iwana must wash and iron and attend to the old Archbishop for all he endless vestments too. Rising at the crack of dawn to grind the coffee and put it to boil, squeeze the oranges and bake the magdalenas for breakfast. Then she must heat the water with aromatic leaves for the bath of María Penitencia, sponging down she broad shoulders, she shiny coconut-head. Then Iwana must prepare the baths for the two daughters, washing and drying and combing out they hair, before she could attend them to dress theyselves. Then – before she could even have a chance to catch she breath – she must take off running across the square to attend the old Archbishop, that by the time those three Marías arrived he could begin the six o'clock Mass. So on and so forth the whole day long, until at last Iwana could descend the stairs to she little room in the basement, followed close behind by María Penitencia, the big key in she hand to lock her up inside. Because of course, that was the only way to keep out Don Antonio. And by the time Iwana lay sheself at last in she little hammock in the corner, and she closed she eyes to drop quiet asleep, María Penitencia was there already at the door unlocking it to let her out.

Now the time arrived for Don Antonio to look for suitable husbands to marry off the two Marías. By now, of course, Demerara was a busy town well known in Europe, and attracting plenty youngmen to come to the Caribbean and make theyselves a fortune. On top of that Fernando de Berrío was convinced that any day soon he would find he El Dorado, and when that happened, of course, everybody would have more gold than they could dream. But in truth the majority of these youngmen coming to Demerara didn't have so much of pedigree and high breeding, but they were only wadjanks and badjohns looking to get theyselves rich. Prisoners that escaped the jail, and thieves, and every kind of scoundrel that you could imagine, that in truth none of those youngmen were suitable for the daughters of Don Antonio a-tall. There was only one, and he was the young French doctor who arrived in Corpus Christi from he city of Marseille. Only boasting about how he was the last of a long long line of Compts, and Bis-Compts, Barons and every kind of thing – and people used to go to hear him recite the names without interruption for three hours at a stretch – tracing he blueblood all the way back to Charlemagne the Great! He full name was *Dr Jewels Derrière-Cri de Plus-Bourbon*. But people used to call him Dr Jewels. So Don Antonio proclaimed that whichever one of the two Marías Dr Jewels chose would go with half he estate, and the other could return to Spain and marry sheself off to the convent.

So for a period of several months Dr Jewels would come every evening to take he dinner at the palace of Don Antonio. But Dr Jewels was famous in Corpus Christi for another thing besides he name, and that was he peculiar culinary habits. You see, the only thing he blueblood would allow him to drink was French champagne – that would be obvious enough – and the only dish he palate could tolerate was the legs of a frog, sauteed soft in butter. Of course, nobody had never even thought of eating those crapolegs before, that people said was surely food for the devil. And it was several evenings before the three Marías and Don Antonio could sit at the same table, watching Dr Jewels nibbling careful at them like little twigs, and not run in the yard quick quick to vomit up they *own* dinner. He would eat them one by one for hours at a stretch – the big red-and-white checkered kerchief tied like the bib of an infant around he neck – he eyes closed tight in complete ecstasy, he fingers and he waxed moustaches dripping with butter. But this vision of Dr Jewels at table was not even the worst thing about all these crapolegs, which of course would require a great quantity piled on the plate as tall as he *nose* to satisfy this Dr Jewels. The worst thing was that now, in addition to all she many *other* labours in the palace, now Iwana must spend several hours a day at that stinking Maraval Swamp, wading through the mud high as she waist, chasing behind all this multitude of jumping crapos. Then she must take out the froglegs and sautee them soft in the butter every evening, that every evening they could be ready in time for the dinner of this Dr Jewels.

After dinner he would take he snifter of cognac and smoke he cigar with Don Antonio. Then he would choose one of the two Marías – Dolores or Consuelo – and they would go and sit together on the back gallery, gazing up at the big moon floating above a glittering sea. Holding hands and reciting poems and professing they love to eachother – all the things that young-people did when they went courting – with of course, María Penitencia the chaperone always there beside them. Some evenings Dr Jewels would go for a walk along the wharf with María Dolores, or he would stroll through a sleeping Demerara arm-in-arm with María Consuelo, with of course, María Penitencia stumbling in the dark a few steps behind.

Soon the day arrived for Dr Jewels to announce he decision. So Don Antonio made a big fête in the palace to celebrate this event, and he invited all the important people of Demerara, including Fernando de Berrío heself. Because he had the ill-fortune to be in port at this same time, furnishing he fleet with fresh supplies. Early that Saturday morning the seamstress brought the gowns for the three Marías, white lace for María Consuelo and red for María Dolores, and of course, black for the gown and the big wide-brimmed hat of María Penitencia. With the three of them fussing the whole day long to get they-selves ready – the two daughters scurrying back and forth in

the palace, each bubbling with excitement sheself – each convinced that *she* would be the choice of the young Dr Jewels.
María Consuelo swore that in the moment of she passion one
evening of sweltering poetry, the eloquent Dr Jewels – *even*
with he mouth full – had pledged heself to her. And María
Dolores proclaimed that just at she climax of he serenade one
slippery and passionate night – poor Dr Jewels with he tongue
in tatters – had promised heself forever to *her*. With Iwana running behind them both from the dawn of morning, bathing
them and combing out they hair and attending them to dress in
they magnificent gowns, and of course, she must prepare all
the food for this big banquet tonight too.

Well those guests consumed a galleon-load of French champagne before the food could even reach the tables. And after
they ate they first and second and they third courses – and then
Iwana brought in the main course which, for Dr Jewels, was
nothing more than he plate of froglegs piled up as tall as he
nose – of course, the rest of those guests had to run in the yard
quick quick to vomit up they *own* previous three courses. But
after all that confusion, and revelry, and so on and so forth –
when they could no longer sustain they suspense and everybody began to beat they spoons against they champagne
glasses – at last Dr Jewels arose to ascend to the podium and
announce he decision. But at that precise moment all they
heard was the big explosion of cannons firing, everybody
burying theyselves beneath the tables. Because of course, when
Sir Walter heard the rumour that de Berrío was returning
home to port for this big fête, he decided it could only mean
they were celebrating he discovery of El Dorado at last. So of
course he had to come straight away with he own fleet of ships,
and launch another of he attacks on unsuspecting Demerara.
He waited until the fête was in full swing, with all those soldiers so borracho they could hardly stand, and he fired off he

cannons all together. But Sir Walter realized soon enough that de Berrío didn't find a fart again as usual – and the only treasure he could think in he moment of frustration to run off with was those two prize daughters of Don Antonio – both they magnificent gowns ruined with the stains of squids simmering in they own ink, both trembling with fear beneath the table.

So now de Berrío had to jump up quick and take off in he fleet chasing behind Raleigh, all the way up the Orinoco again, and attack him and take back the two prize Marías. Of course, now there was the same great preoccupation weighing down on everybody's mind, particular Don Antonio's and Doña Penitencia's. Because nobody really believed what they said about those English sailors, even after the evidence to document the proof. That it didn't have nothing to do with all they boasting about honour – all they feathers, and flowery gestures, and all they schoolgirl manners – because every single Englishman is a fairyboy in truth.

It was Dr Jewels heself who performed those inspections. Utilizing the probe of he own educated little finger, with all Demerara waiting anxious outside the palace to hear the results. And before long he appeared gallant on the balcony to drape he kerchief over the rail – not the checkered one, but a special *white* kerchief this time – and then he retrieved the kerchief to repeat heself draping it over the rail a *second* time, the whole crowd bursting forth spontaneous in a great uproar. Because of course, this was the signal obvious enough for everybody to understand, that *both* those Marías still possessed they virtues untouched. Except of course by the Doctor's own little finger.

Don Antonio was so pleased he declared a festival to last for three days and nights. Everybody singing, and dancing, and drinking rum in the streets – that many people say how this is the true origin of modern day carnival – and when at last they were all exhausted, and stale-drunk, all with they voices hoarse from so much bacchanal, they dragged theyselves once again to assemble beneath the balcony of Don Antonio. Now Dr Jewels appeared again to announce he decision everybody was waiting in suspense for so long to hear, which of those two Marías he would choose for he wife, and which would return to Spain to bury sheself in the convent? But no sooner could he open he mouth when a *next* spontaneous uproar arose from the crowd – this time of cursing, and beating they fists in the air, and pelting rotten fruit – because what Dr Jewels answered, in all he youthful innocence, was that he didn't understand the question.

You see, just like all those sophisticated young Frenchmen of polish, and education, and plenty pretensions during that era, this Dr Jewels was a Socialist. That means of course he was an atheist too – and he didn't believe in Papa God, nor Pope nor King nor nothing else a-tall besides the power of *money* – so how could he *possibly* marry heself to a Roman Catholic like either of those two Marías? Dr Jewels said, just as you are expecting, that if Don Antonio still wanted him for he son-in-law, then the only way was for him to marry he *youngest* daughter, who was none other than the Princess Iwana. Because even though from a little girl Iwana had spent all she time in the church, running behind the old Archbishop, it never occurred to none of them even to pelt a little holywater and a pinch of salt over she head to baptize her. So before Don Antonio and Doña Penitencia could have a chance to think how they could get theyselves out from this pepperpot they'd found theyselves swimming in all of a sudden, the crowd let loose another spontaneous explosion of *cheering* this time. And just like true blue Caribbean people, they took off for another three days of carnival and bacchanal in the streets. Leaving Don Antonio and those three Marías standing there

135

on the balcony, all cross-eyed with they mouths hanging wide
open like if *they* were a family of lizards now catching flies.

So first thing Dr Jewels had to build a house adequate for heself
and Iwana to live in, and he built the biggest one, on the highest point of the whole island. It was a *castle* bigger than Sand-
lord's own, bigger even than the palace of Don Antonio. With
walls that were five feet thick of solid coral blocks, and it had
more than a hundred rooms, each with a window looking out
over the sea. And the bedroom of Dr Jewels had its own fire-
place – a big bed with the canopy above, and a bathtub with the
golden feet of a lion below – and hidden behind the bookcase
in the library was a secret door. That door opened to a narrow
hallway with a deep dark hole at the end, like a waterwell
without the water, and a long ladder to climb down inside.
Then a tunnel to crawl on hands and knees all the way beneath
the foundations of the castle, then a stone staircase winding
around and around climbing higher and higher, until you
reached to the highest point of the roof. Then there was a next
door of rusty iron bars and a big rusty padlock, and of course,
beyond this second door was the tower of this castle. It was
open to the open air, only a piece of thatched roof in the corner,
and beneath the roof was the bed. Only a little bed with a
prickly coconut-fibre mattress, and attached to one leg of the
bed was a long rusty chain. At the other end of this chain – with
a next padlock and a rusty neck-clamp clasping secure around
she neck – was of course Iwana, sitting naked on the little bed.
But Iwana was happier living in the tower of that castle than
she had been in all she life!

Now she didn't have that household of Don Antonio to take
care of, with those three Marías and the old Archbishop to run
behind from dawn of morning until late into the night. Now

she didn't have she cold dark cell in the basement to sleep the stingy few minutes Doña Penitencia would allow her at the end of she wretched days. Because in truth, there wasn't nothing in the world Iwana loved to do better than *sleep!* Now she would crawl out from under she piece of thatched roof to stretch sheself lazy beneath the sun, she skin a glittering gold, eyes half-closed beneath she thick dreamy lids. The whole day long, not even a worry in the world! And she never felt lonely nor hungry neither, because from that first day in the tower iguana came to visit her.

Understand, there beside this castle was the tallest and oldest tree on the whole island. And Johnny, this ain't no beanstalk we're talking about! This one was a giant *kapok* tree, the royal silk cotton, with the tallest of its branches hanging just above the piece of thatched roof. Iguana – who was the only creature on Papa God's earth able to climb so high – iguana would drop from out the tree to land safe with a *thwack* on the thatched roof, and she would go to visit with Iwana. That first morning iguana happened to be chewing the last piece of a soft green dasheen leaf, she favourite food, and of course, Iwana's eyes lit up straight away. She hadn't seen a tender dasheen leaf like that since she was a little girl. That same night was a fullmoon night, and early the following morning iguana brought her a big bundle of leaves tied together with twine. With the two of them chewing happy together the *whole* day long – pausing every now and again only to stretch out side-by-side for a nap beneath the sun – both they eyes half-closed beneath they dreamy lids. Until late one afternoon, with the sun sinking slow in the glittering sea beneath a crimson sky, when they were startled awake by the rattling of Dr Jewels in the padlock.

Iguana didn't have no choice, and neither did Iwana. There wasn't even time to scramble beneath the bed and hide sheself.

Because of course, like everybody else on the island, iguana had long ago heard about the peculiar palate of this Dr Jewels. And Johnny, the tail of an iguana doesn't taste so different from the legs of a crapo a-tall! In the space of a breath Iwana had stretched out one of she long golden legs toward iguana, and iguana scrambled up quick along it, disappearing sudden inside!

But as much as everybody on the island knew about the unusual *culinary* habits of this French doctor, nobody had never heard nothing before about he peculiar palate for sex. And that was a fortunate thing for both iguana and Iwana. Because if he did he business normal like everybody else as you would expect, Dr Jewels would have discovered iguana hiding inside Iwana straight away. But Johnny, in order to par-take of *he* particular kind of pleasure, Dr Jewels didn't even need to take off he clothes. On the contrary, he dressed heself up in more clothes, if you consider the big red-and-white checkered kerchief he took out from he back pocket, and he tied it up like the bib of an infant around he neck. Now Dr Jew-els took hold of the rusty chain attached to the neck-clamp around Iwana's neck, and he led her over to the little bed. But he didn't do it rough, nor brute, nor in any way cruel! Because the truth is that despite that rusty chain – despite the padlock and neck-clamp and all the rest – this Dr Jewels always hand-led Iwana like if she was a china doll. Like if she was a fragile little bird, and he put her to sit gentle on the bed, she back rest-ing cool against the coral wall. Now Dr Jewels opened up she legs. He went down on he knees beside the bed as if he was no longer the socialist-atheist a-tall, but he was a better Catholic than all of us, only preparing heself to say he evening prayers. As if he was sitting at table before he cherished plate of froglegs sauteed soft in butter – and he smoothed back he stiff mous-taches with he eyes closed tight in complete ecstasy just the same – Dr Jewels bent over careful beneath Iwana for he evening feast.

Papa-yo! What Dr Jewels tasted, of course, was not Iwana, but *iguana*, hiding sheself inside Iwana. And of course, he'd never tasted a pussy so *sweet* as that in all he life! Because this Dr Jewels, due to he medical profession, had the opportunity to study a great variety. And he'd sampled every thinkable flavour and nationality, from French Bordeau, to Italian oregano, to English pussies doused in they double cream. Hindu palori pussies, German pussies boiled in beer, and Portugee cavinadash pussies pickled in garlic. This Dr Jewels had the opportunity to sample Chinee sideways pussies, Singapore squinty-eye ones – even the incense-smoking *Catholic* pussies of those two Marías – since this particular preference of Dr Jewels was the only *un*perilous kind of sex condoned by the Church. But Johnny, he had never before tasted nothing like Iwana, who in truth was iguana.

And so every evening it was just the same. Soon as the sun began to sink beneath the sea, and iguana and Iwana heard the rattling of Dr Jewels with he key in the gate. Iguana would scramble up she leg and hide sheself inside Iwana. And Dr Jewels would take out he red-and-white checkered bib from he back pocket, and he would go down on he knees beside the bed for he evening feast. But Johnny, it is only fair to Dr Jewels to tell you that after a time, Iwana had learned to close she eyes just the same. After a time *Iwana* discovered she pleasures in those evening visits of Dr Jewels too. Until she could no longer tolerate the intensity of she own excitement, and she would shove he head tender away. And Dr Jewels, always kind and respectful of Iwana, would wipe he whiskers and fold up he bib again straight away in he back pocket, he would bow he head gallant before her, and he would hurry out the gate.

Every evening it was just the same, as I was saying. And almost before Iwana could realize the years had passed. But hidden away like that high in the tower of this castle, Iwana could never know of the happenings of the world at she feet. Of course, iguana would keep her informed to a certain extent, and she brought her fresh news every morning. Of the most recent events in Demerara, of the latest attacks of Sir Walter on Fernando de Berrío, of de Berrío's retaliations on Sir Walter Raleigh. But there was one piece of news iguana could never find the heart to tell Iwana. It was news of she own Amerindian people, of she royal family at home, of the Arawacks, and Caribs, and Warrahoons. Of how all those Europeans were killing them off fast enough. Putting them as slaves to grow the cane and make the sugar – and tobacco, coffee, cocoa and *all* they crops – and they worked those gentle Amerindians and beat them with the cat-of-the-nine-tails until they dropped. Iguana could never find the heart to tell Iwana that in truth, all she royal family had perished long ago, and there wasn't a handful of she people still walking the earth. Because Johnny, already those Europeans were bringing shiploads of *new* slaves to this Caribbean. New ones to replace the perished Amerindians. These slaves came on ships from *Africa*. And iguana never told Iwana that even in the castle of Dr Jewels, there wasn't but a single Amerindian slave remaining. Now they all were Africans.

Dr Jewels *heself* began to change, as if to coincide with all these changes of the world. By now this Dr Jewels had become a rickety oldman, frustrated with heself and he own feeble oldage. He no longer treated Iwana so kind, nor gentle, and Johnny, some of he activities during this period were too nasty to name. Iwana and iguana soon came to *despise* he visits each afternoon. Then, one afternoon with no warning a-tall, Dr Jewels appeared in the tower accompanied by another. It was the first time in *all* those years he had not arrived alone. This time – attached to a next rusty chain with a next neck-clamp and padlock – Dr Jewels brought with him the new slaveboy he'd purchased that same morning in the market. And Johnny, when Iwana heard the rattling of Dr Jewels in the padlock that afternoon, and she opened she half-closed lids to see the creature standing there beside him, *now* she sat up straight away. Because Iwana had never seen a man so *beautiful* as him in all she life! Similar to Iwana, this young slaveboy was a prince from the royal family of he own Yoruba people. Tall and strong with rich purple skin and the grace of a panther moving beneath the trees, a gentle look on he face, and he name was *Anaconda*.

Dr Jewels took out he red-and-white kerchief just the same. He went down on he knees at the bedside before Iwana, just as he did every evening. But this time he held in he hands the chain of Anaconda, standing there beside him with he head turned to look the other way. Because of course, he would never look at Iwana to shame her so. *Never!* And now – when Dr Jewels had satisfied heself and he folded up he kerchief again in he back pocket – now he *didn't* bow he head gallant to take he leave as usual. Johnny, now this wicked Dr Jewels wanted the *additional* pleasure of observing Anaconda, doing what he, in he feeble oldage, could never manage heself. He commanded Anaconda to strip heself naked. Anaconda obeyed. He order him to lay heself on the bed beside Iwana. And Anaconda lay heself down. Now Dr Jewels smiled wicked and he smoothed back he waxed moustaches, and he ordered Anaconda to kiss Iwana. First she mouth, and then she soft breasts. Anaconda obeyed. But quick as Dr Jewels could issue the next *in*human command – Iwana trembling with fear in Anaconda's strong arms, frightened for both sheself *and* iguana – Anaconda took

141

pity, and he called up those special powers that he had brought with him across the sea from Africa.

Johnny, just like all those Yoruba princes of royal African blood, Anaconda could change he shape at will to the very creature that bore he name. And in that same instant, Iwana looked down to discover only the thick black snake squirming on the bed beside her. With Dr Jewels standing there astonished, nothing in he hands but the rusty chain and the empty neck-clamp! Quick as a breath Anaconda climbed up onto the piece of thatched roof above they heads, up onto the nearest branch of that kapok tree. Because despite the fact that Anaconda could never climb *up* a tree so tall, he could climb down easy enough! Dropping one branch to the next until he reached safe to the ground. And then – the most curious thing of all – Anaconda crawled straight into the waiting crocusssack of Dr Jewels. Because of course, Dr Jewels had hurried heself back down the stairs, and he was there waiting beneath the tree to hold Anaconda prisoner again.

It happened the same way every evening, time and time again. Anaconda taking he animal shape and sliding away at the last minute, with Dr Jewels hurrying down from the tower to capture him again – of he *own* volition – as soon as Anaconda could reach the ground. Until one evening when the sun was just disappearing beneath the glittering sea, the whole sky burning a bright crimson, and Anaconda could never resist the temptation to pause there on the branch a moment to take it in. Then he turned to watch Dr Jewels hurrying out the tower gate, rusty chain and neck-clamp dragging down the stairs behind him. And then – so strange a sight he had to blink he eyes twice before he could *believe* it – Anaconda watched iguana wriggle sheself out from inside Iwana. He shook he head, and he was

142

just about to write it off as another one of those meaningless, magical events common enough in folktale-stories like this – ready to drop down to the next branch and begin he descent again – when he happened to see something else to sadden he heart: the two of them were weeping. So now Anaconda dropped instead with a *thwack* back to the piece of roof, and he slid down the post again to question them why.

They both answered together, Iwana and iguana, speaking both at the same time. And they told him, of course, that they were both in love with him. Each, of course, with the appropriate shape. Anaconda looked up at the crimson sky a moment, and filled with sadness heself, he told them that he, too, was very much in love. To such extent that he was willing to surrender heself a prisoner to Dr Jewels every evening, only to enjoy the kisses of beautiful Iwana again. An *impossible* love! But just as soon as he said this a spark lit up in the depths of Anaconda's dark eyes. He smiled, and he told them both to dry they tears. 'Let me study me head *good* tonight,' he said. 'And tomorrow evening, I going to tell you what we will do!' With that Anaconda slid up onto the thatched roof, he climbed up onto the nearest branch, and he began he descent down the great kapok. Down toward the ready crocusssack of Dr Jewels.

The following evening Anaconda waited for Dr Jewels to take he leave as usual. Again he dropped with a *thwack* to the piece of roof, and he slid down toward Iwana and iguana, a smile shining on he face. 'Listen!' he told them both. 'What I going to do is take off my skin. And I want iguana to put it on. Tomorrow, when Dr Jewels comes to take he feast, iguana must crawl up inside Iwana just the same. *Then*,' Anaconda said, smiling he knowing smile, 'we going to see what we will see!'

And that was just what happened. Anaconda took off he long skin, and he slid away blushing like a little boy. But Anaconda's skin was a size many *many* times too long to fit iguana.

143

She put it on just the same. And just as you would suppose too – all those ages and ages ago when the earth was young sheself – iguana was still a fresh younggirl. She skin as soft and smooth as a new zabuca-pear, golden and glistening without a blemish to the tip of she tail! But Johnny, by the time iguana finished dressing sheself in Anaconda's long skin, she didn't look like no springchicken *a-tall*. Now she looked like the oldest ramshackled creature on all Papa God's earth! Like a ratty old rastaman, he dreadlocks hanging down below he waist, so many wrinkles did iguana have now around she neck, she belly and all about. *So* many wrinkles that she had to struggle and struggle to squeeze all that extra skin inside Iwana, the following afternoon when Dr Jewels arrived with Anaconda, he big key rattling inside the gate.

After only a single sour taste of *Anaconda*, Dr Jewels opened he eyes wide wide for the first time ever during he evening feasts. He looked inside Iwana to see all those endless oldlady wrinkles, in that very pussy which only the previous day, he had tasted smooth, and sweet, fresh as a fresh younggirl! Dr Jewels jumped up in a rage straight away. He rushed to the wall of the tower to spit the sour taste over the side. And Johnny, then something happened that nobody could anticipate a-tall. Even me, and I have been telling this story for so many years. Now Dr Jewels turned around to see beautiful Iwana lying there on the bed, handsome Anaconda there at the bedside also – two of the most *beautiful* creatures ever to walk on Papa God's golden earth – and he saw for the first time the reality of those wretched chains around they necks. He contemplated for the first time the wretched state that was the world – which, in good measure, was he *own* doing – and without the least forewarning a-tall, Dr Jewels threw heself from the tower to he death down below.

Just like that! The story was over already, before anybody

144

was ready to see it finish. Because Johnny, the only thing remaining was for iguana to crawl out from inside Iwana, so Anaconda could make love to her for we tale to have its happy end. But then something *else* happened that neither of those three, nor nobody else could have ever suspected. You see, when iguana wriggled sheself out from Iwana at last, she couldn't help but leave half the wrinkled up skin inside. And when iguana tried to wriggle out *sheself* from all that wrinkled up skin she was wearing, she *couldn't*. All that skin had stuck - to Iwana and iguana – and so *both* of them remained with they wrinkles to this very day. It's true, that's the way they got them. And Johnny, when you grow older and you have the opportunity to look for youself, you'll find all those wrinkles folded up inside just the same. Just as I am telling you. But don't worry, because Johnny, one more thing that I can tell you about iguanas too – *despite* all they wrinkles – is that both of them remained young and sweet sweet forever!

This, of course, Anaconda knew as good as anybody else. So with the sun just disappearing beneath the glittering sea, all the sky above them painted a brilliant crimson, Iwana and Anaconda could make love to each other at last. And the next morning, Anaconda taught her the trick of how to change she shape. Iwana *became* iguana. Then Anaconda changed to he serpent self too, both of them climbing down from the giant kapok tree. They disappeared inside the forest, where they have lived happy together to this very day. Only on occasion, when the moon is full with the scent of the forest green like the first day Papa God breathed life in the earth, do Anaconda and Iwana feel a longing to change they shape. Only on occasion do they surrender, and only to make love together like human beings.

5

Further Adventures of the Kentucky Colonel and the King of Chacachacari, and How My Grandmother Became a Disk-Jockey and the First Female Calypsonian, and Managed by Accident to Decode a German Message so America Could Win the War

Let me tell you Johnny, the only thing to attract more trouble than a young widow with *plenty* good looks like I had in those days, and beautiful beautiful tot-tots that didn't used to fall down, is when you've got a few cents tied up in the kerchief hiding between them. And the only thing more dangerous than one scoundrel chasing you tail behind you, is when you turn around to find *two*. That was when the war was fighting still, with the American Base they built in Chaguarameras still the biggest confusion ever to descend on this island. Everybody going around the place with they mouths twisted up saying one set of foolishness like *You becha!* and *How-dee-do!* because all we needed was a few of those big hats to convince us we were *all* living in a cowboy picture with John Wayne. I still had the boarding house there on Rust Street for five or six of the young American soldiers to stay with me, that after a time those boys came to replace my own sons away studying in Canada – all except for you daddy and you Uncle Amadao – with those soldiers treating me and Gregoria la Rosa like we were they own adopted mummies too.

So that afternoon Gregoria cooked a giant tattoo that the boys could take for they dinner. Because that thing was as big as *you*, Johnny – five feet from head to tail that I don't know how she even fit it inside the oven – as those soldiers were always excited for us to give them some new West Indian dish for them to try.

Now Gregoria said she wanted to decorate him with some pars-
ley beneath he arms, and pry open he pointy mouth to push a
governor's plum inside. I told her she could shove a carrot up he
culo if she wanted, and she could dress him in a tuxedo with a
mariposa bowtie and Uncle Sam tophat but he would still be a
tattoo, and only a tattoo, and nothing more than a tattoo, but
whatever it was she better do it *quick*, because those boys would
be arriving hungry from the Base beating they fists against the
table any minute. Two of us were there in the kitchen arguing
together happy enough, when all in a sudden we heard one set
of noise coming from in front the house, so Gregoria and me
took off running to find out what was going on.

Just there in the middle of the frontyard was a big crowd of
people gathered around this chuff-chuff man with he long grey
beard. Only thing he wasn't wearing no clothes a-tall except
for a sheet wrapped around him like the diaper of a baby, and
he was sitting at the top of he pram that was a kind of a golden
donkeycart, or one of them *kickshaws* like they have in Japan.
But instead of the single human-donkey he had a whole tribe of
six or eight baboo-boys dressed in they diapers too – each one
biting down on the donkey-bridle between he teeth, each
attached to the reins of this whiteman cracking he whip to
drive them along – with the pile of he grey Samsonite suitcases
in a heap on the kickshaw behind him.

Well! Gregoria and me had never seen nothing like this
before, not even for Dimanche Gras on Carnival Sunday. Now
I heard Gregoria whisper, 'Oui fute! It's the West Indian rendition of Father Christmas!' I said, 'Either that, or it's Papa God
heself come to pay us a visit in he golden chariot of baboo-
angels!' But when I studied this man good a moment – with the
white turban wrapped around he head and the ruby upon he
forehead flashing, and he big stomach spilling out with a *next*
ruby big as you fist like this shoved up inside he bellyhole –

now I realized that sheet wasn't no baby diaper a-tall, it was the 'ceremonial gown'. Because even though he'd grown out the long grey beard, and he'd given up he pirogue for the donkeycart-kickshaw with those same baboo-boys to tote him, sure enough he was the identical King. Now I informed Gregoria all excited, 'Neither Father Christmas, nor Papa God, nor even a Julius Caesar that needs to put heself on a serious diet. It's my good old friend, the King of Chacachacari!'

Of course, Gregoria wasn't living in the house then, and she only pushed a chups to ask where was this *Chacachacari* place that she'd never heard nothing about it before, but I didn't even waste my breath to explain, because by then I was already running out to greet the King! But before I could even have a chance to open my mouth he clapped he hands twice together – *bam bam* – and straight away one of the little baboos spat out he bridle to take off running around behind the King, and he pulled down a big Samsonite suitcase to present it to me. Now the King announced in a loud voice, 'This, good Madame, is a token of we great veneration and affection vouchsafed from we distant country across the sea!' Of course, I was trembling with excitement now thinking this suitcase was surely stuffed to the brim with shining rubies, or gold coins, or some treasure so, but when I twisted the latches to throw it open all I found inside was the pile of dirty old underdrawers, and Johnny, they weren't smelling so good neither!

Then I realized this was only the King's sense of humour, and beneath those shitty drawers was bound to be a twelve carat diamond, but when I closed my eyes to plunge my hand in it wasn't the glittering diamond I pulled out a-tall. It was a funny black instrument shaped like an overgrown one of those saucers they put for the tourists to play they shuffleboards – except it had the electric cord dangling – with the circle of indentations going around the top like somebody scooped them out with a soupspoon. Of course, the King saw the look of perplexion on my face, which sent him into a fit of laughing out loud, and he told me to try and guess what it was. I told him it was either a telephone to talk to the man in the moon, or Papa God's own mould for making *cojones*. Now the King laughed some more, and he told me I was close enough the second time, that it was a special machine for cooking *poached* eggs. *Well!* I was a little bit disappointed to hear this, as so far as *I* was concerned he fancy machine wasn't worth a fart. Because I knew everything there was to know about fowl eggs – chicken and pigeon and guineyhen – and I had eaten iguana eggs, and caiman eggs, mappapee and macajuel and every kind of eggs belonging to a tortoise – marocoy and leatherback and hawksbill – but I didn't even know what the ass kind of animal was this *poach*, less still where to find its nest. Of course, I didn't want to seem a spoilfish so I painted the big smile across my face just the same, and I told the King how pleased I was and thank you very much, and welcome, and I hope he and he little boys could stay and take they dinner with us tonight as we were serving a tattoo big enough to feed he *entire* kingdom of Chacachacari! The King said that would be very fine, as there ain't nothing he liked to eat better than a tasty tattoo.

But before he could even get a chance to dismount from out he donkeycart-kickshaw a big white motorcar pulled to a screeching halt in the middle of all of us standing there in the frontyard, with the cloud of dust rolling from behind to send us choking. And when the air cleared for us to make out this big Cadillac with the top that folded itself up and down – the fins and flippers and the two wings pushing out from the sides like a flyingfish out the water – sure enough sitting there in the front seat was none other than the real life Kentucky Colonel, and sitting beside him of course was he partner-in-crime, the same old Tanzanian Devil! So I could only think that when it rains it

149

surely pours to soak you down to you pantyhose, and now I was rushing around to the other side of this motorcar to greet the Colonel, as I hadn't seen *him* in such a long time neither!

But when I looked again he was no longer even sitting behind the wheel. In a single leap he threw heself out of the front seat to pounce right on top the poor King – and he pulled him down on the ground rolling in a lockgrip like two bubulups little badjohns wrestling in the schoolyard – with all the crowd letting loose they spontaneous explosion of laughing, and bawling, and clapping they hands together, because they'd never seen two grown whitemen carrying on like this in all they lives! Next thing you know they started cuffing each other up – but fortunate for us the boys arrived just in time from the Base, they own Jeep screeching to a halt – and in no time they pulled them apart and doused them each with a bucket of water to cool them down. Now I had to reprimand the Colonel that he should be *ashamed* of heself, that the poor King only just arrived behaving heself proper enough, so why did the Colonel have to pounce on top him like a wild Warrahoon fresh out the bush that don't got no education, nor manners, nor good breeding? But the Colonel only busied heself emptying one by one the pockets of he white pantaloons and he jacket – because they were all puffed up now like a suit of miniature hotwater bottles – he fixed the little black ribbon tied in a bow around he neck for the tie, and he slipped he goldwatch on the chain dangling back inside he vestcoat pocket.

Now he cleared he throat preparing for this big speech, and he told me, 'Skip, this here *King* standing before you ain't nothing more than a belly-slivering snake. He's a rat-scampering rascal, a rogue, and an eater of tinned beats. A brassfaced, bigmouthed, blue-striped, balloon-bellied son-of-a-peacock, and he's got lilies in he liver and quaileggs inside he pants. He's a frufru, a beggar, a thousand-pound pussywillow that don't remember the last time he showered with soap nor sprayed deodorant beneath he arms. All this and plenty more, Skip, and I will bust him in he catfish-kisser if he tries to subtract the least addition.'

Papa-yo! Now the crowd let loose they cry of cheering again, and now it was the *King* who raised up he hand slow in the air to silence them. 'My good Madame,' he said, 'please excuse my French. But if the Colonel here could pause a moment to pull he dung-dubbed dipstick out the hindquarters of every little boychild in the whole of Christendom, he could gaze in the lookglass and know heself. Nothing less than the fattest, flabbiest, pulpy-fleshed, milk-dripping, banana-peeling fruit-of-a-soursop ever to stuff heself into a three piece suit. He's the daughter of he prostitute father, and the mother of he whoresome son. He cherished game is pin the male in he donkey-tail, and he favourite military dish is lick-the-privates-clean-please. All this and more besides, my goodliest Madame, and the worst part of him is the smell of he afterslave.'

Well! the crowd only let loose they explosion of bawling and cheering again, and I could only think of *one* way to put a stop to this Elizabethan tournament of caca-pelting going on in we own frontyard one time and finish. Straight away I pulled my little pearlhandled pistol out from between my tot-tots, I pointed it up in the air to fire two times

pa-pow! pa-pow!

and everybody dropped to a dead quiet. I said that listening to them two was worse than watching the Olympics pingpong match between Hitler and Sir Winston Churchill in truth, so before we have a World War *III* on we hands let's put a lid on both they yakers right now – because of course I had to give it to them in they own Yankee-cowboy language that they could understand – and now I paused a moment as dramatic as the

Duke heself, and I blew away the smoke from the end of my pearlhandled pistol!

The crowd realized this was the end of all they fun and games for one afternoon – because they knew me good enough that I didn't put up with no bub-ball in *my* house – and they could just as well carry theyselves home to they own dinner. Now I told the Colonel and he partner Tanzania that I was pleased to see them too, and they were welcome to take they dinner with us, everybody together like one big happy family, because we were eating a tattoo tonight fat enough to feed he entire Confederate Army! The Colonel said he'd never eaten *tattoo* before – but so long as it was coming from *Skip's* kitchen it was bound to taste sweeter than a Burbon Street lobsteress in she pretty pink garters – and he would try he best to behave heself and no more cursing and misbehaving. I made the King and the Colonel shake hands together, and we were all happy as we could be, and now I announced at last what everybody was waiting anxious to hear, 'Time to hit the grits!'

So we all assembled weself around the big diningroom table – all except for those baboo-boys belonging to the King that there wasn't chairs enough for them too – but we promised to send them out the dinner straight away. Now Gregoria la Rosa brought in this tattoo that was so big she could hardly tote him, all dressed up fancy as a Christmas pig on he silver platter, and she put him down in the middle of the table. But now everybody dropped silent a moment because they were *sure* they'd never seen no animal like this before, that it looked to them like a survivor from the age of the dinosaurs, and they didn't know what he was. Then all in a sudden the Colonel exclaimed in a loud voice, 'Sweet succupus! I do believe that there creature is a *armadiller!*' and the boys all started nodding they heads in recognition, and they yelled out together in a chorus of 'Hot dog!' I told them they could call him *succupus*, or *armadiller*, or *hot dog*, or whatever the ass they wanted. But the *true* name was *tattoo* because that was what the Arawack Indians called him, a thousand years before there even *was* an America to take over not only the English language, but all the rest besides. Of course, what I *didn't* bother to explain to them was how in the language of those Arawacks this name actually meant 'it ain't worth a fart', since those Indians had *plenty* better things to eat than a hardback tattoo. Because of course, the biggest problem about eating this animal was how the ass to crack open he shell and get at the meat inside? But just as I was thinking this Gregoria came in from the backyard carrying she cutlass like if she was going out to the fields to chop cane, and she raised up the long blade high as the chandelier up above we heads, ready to bring it down on the back of this tattoo.

All in a sudden the King bawled out '*Halt!*' and he told us that in he kingdom of Chacachacari they happened to be living in *this* century, and they were plenty more sophisticated and modernized than that. Then he put he two fingers in he mouth to let loose a shrill whistle, and straight away one of the little baboos came running with another funny instrument like some kind of mechanical scissors, the long cord trailing behind. Now the King announced just as you are expecting that this machine was the 'electric tattoo-opener' – that in addition it worked very well to open tin cans – and the King put he machine on the table and plugged it in. He clamped down the lever of he tattoo-opener just behind the little pointy ear, he pressed a button and he machine came to life making a noise like if it was gargling saltwater. Now the King turned the big platter in a slow circle with he tattoo-opener gargling away. *Oui fute, papa-yo!* The King pressed the button to silence he machine, he pushed open the lever, and now he lifted off the entire back of this tattoo easy as one of those same soldiers taking off he field helmet!

Of course, we were all mesmerized by this miracle of modern science taking place before we own eyes, and we couldn't help but clap we hands together in a round of applause. The King bowed he head and took he seat again, and now I could begin to carve the tattoo up with Gregoria passing around the plates. The boys all said how this was surely something to write home about – that we had served them this prehistoric animal to eat – and of course the Tanzanian Devil was bound to put in he own nasty two-cents too! He said yes, but what he was *really* looking forward to was a couple of those rosy ripe mammy-apples for dessert, and with that he reached out he two hands to give Gregoria's tot-tots a squeeze. Sweet heart of Jesus! Gregoria let loose a scream to drop the plate of tattoo she was holding and take off running for the kitchen, and I advised Tanzania he'd better behave heself. Because this was a respectable boarding house and not one of those *pussy*clubs like every other on the whole island since the war started, and they arrived with all these sex-starved American boys because where they came from it was against the law even to *play* with youself before the age of twenty-one – and then you had to have a special government license – and I warned Tanzania that the *next* time he tried a stunt like that my pearlhandled pistol would explode he cojones so far apart he would never find them!

Now at last we could all begin to enjoy we tattoo civilized enough, and we piled up a big tall plate for each of those little baboos waiting hungry outside. Let me tell you Johnny, we ate peas-and-rice, ground provisions, buttered christophene, yucca in garlic sauce, and we ate on that tattoo till there was nothing remaining but the carcass of bones connecting the pointy tail with the little squashed head. And even that *tail* the Colonel cracked between he teeth like if it was the claw of a crawdad, and he told us it tasted sweeter than a lady longneck fresh out the wrappers of she blue bayou. And just when we were all thinking we would surely *die* if we tried to swallow another morsel, another grain of rice, Gregoria got up from she chair to go in the kitchen and bring back a guava duff. So of course we each had to have a slice, that when we finished we could only sit there bobo as a table full of bubulupses after this big marathon of eating tattoo, all of us groaning with every now and then one of the boys excusing heself for a little belch, and just like the good old times, the Colonel expressed my permission to press in he little round potbelly a moment to relieve a fart.

But after a few minutes we all recovered weself, and now it was the King who rose to he feet with a little bit of trouble at the head of the table. He cleared he throat, and he announced in a loud voice, 'Ladies and gentlemen, as the proud and privileged guest of honour this evening, I hereby arrest the attentions of all present to partake of the time-old tradition of this hospitable board. So kindly bend all ears in the direction of the good Madame, that she could relate to us one of she famous tales!' Well they all started to clap they hands again, so even though I was exhausted to my bones I didn't have no choice but oblige them with a short one. But now I announced that before I could begin to recount this *particular* tale tonight, we had to beg permission from we own beloved Gregoria la Rosa. Because the fact is that this tale belonged duly to her. But it was *not* a fairytale story of fantasy, and magic, and make-believe talking animals intended only for young children like you were all thinking – it was a *true true* story of adventure, and mischief, and plenty bub-ball – and it took place right here in the very house you are all sitting in right now, not even a year ago, and the title is

Gregoria's Story of the Time She Got the Pin-Cushion Stuck
Inside She Bamsee, and the Good Madame Attempted to Operate
on Her and Almost Pulled Out She Whole Asshole

Of course, Gregoria burst out straight away, 'No, no, Mummy! Please don't tell them that one *again*, it's too embarrassing!' But by now the boys had heard this title with all they imaginations already wet, and it was too late, because they wouldn't settle for *no* other story. Gregoria jumped up in a huff from she place beside me to say that if she had to allow it, at least she didn't have to *hear* it again for the ninety-ninth fucking time, and she disappeared hissing like a wet landcrab inside she hole of the kitchen to wash the wares.

So this story begins on an evening that was just like any other in this house, just like tonight, except instead of the giant tattoo Gregoria had made a big big pot of bull-foot soup that the soldiers could take for they dinner. Gregoria knew good enough that you boys were always excited for us to give you some new West Indian dish to try, and truth is that since the war started a bull-foot was sometimes the closest thing you could pay good money for if you wanted a piece of meat. So Gregoria ladled out the soup passing it all around – with those boys saying just like tonight how *this* was surely something to write home about – that we had served them this soup each one with he own private bull-foot standing up in the middle of the bowl. So we were all sitting there waiting for Gregoria to come back and take she seat so we could begin the dinner, with that soup steaming up and smelling good and all of us so hungry – but Gregoria didn't come back from out the kitchen a-tall – which was very peculiar to me as this soup was one of she favourites. After a time I told the boys they might as well 'chow down', and straight away they all started with they *slup slup slup* and 'Please pass some more of that bull-foot soup!' – everybody happy as a gang of schoolboys traipsing through a puddle of mud – so now I could get up to go and find out what was wrong with Gregoria.

I found her standing at the back of the kitchen in a funny kind of a squat, *weeping* with the big tears rolling down she cheeks, and she was only rubbing up she bamsee groaning groaning like she'd sat down on a stinging nettle bush. And that was just what I told her intending to make a little joke, and I took her in my arms trying my best to console her. But Gregoria only continued to weep, and she told me, '*Plenty* worse than a stinging nettle bush, Mummy! It's the *pin-cushion* I must have sat down on without realizing, and now it's stuck up inside my bamsee!'

Of course, the first thing I asked her logical enough was if she'd checked the sewingbox to make *sure*. She told me not only had she looked there, but she'd turned she bedroom upside-down and searched the whole house, and she couldn't find it nowhere a-tall, and she said that it was bound to be that pin-cushion Mummy, because what else could give her such a terrible terrible pain pinching and poking and plucking like that inside she bamsee?

Well! I was no longer liking the sound of this thing a-tall, since for me there isn't *nothing* so important to appreciate the pleasures of life like a contented culo. No different from enjoying a fancy feast – or listening to a good story like this one you are hearing right now – because it doesn't amount to nothing more than the pile of caca in the chamberpot beneath you bed, if it doesn't come out with the satisfying and happy *end*. That was what I explained to Gregoria as patient and gentle as I could manage, and she hugged me and dried she tears to gave me a little smile, and I told her, 'OK. Now bend over like a good girl and

157

open up you cheeks for me to look inside!' Of course, this only sent her into a fit of bawling again, and she let loose another whelp of pain, and now she told me for the third time, 'No, no, Mummy! Please don't make me do that, it's too embarrassing!'

Sweet heart of Jesus! Only thing I could think to do was to take up the big bowl of macaroni-pie that was waiting there on the counter for the segundo plato, and I carried it out to the boys. By this time of course they had finished they bull-foot soup, and I told them to please help theyselves to some macaroni-pie, and not to worry about Gregoria and me that we had a small emergency in the kitchen. Because Gregoria made the mistake of sitting down on the pin-cushion, and now it was lodged up inside she culo, and I had to find some way to pry it out. Of course, those boys had been living here with Gregoria and me long enough just like you, and they were accustomed every night to little confusions like this in the house. Plus they all knew how Gregoria and me were two women with we hysterical imaginations that sometimes we could get a little bit carried away with weselves, so they didn't pay us hardly no mind, and they went back to enjoying they macaroni-pie. Now I took down the decanter off the shelf where I kept my little brandy, so I could take a nip with my boys every now and again after dinner, and two of those little shot glasses, and I went back to Gregoria thinking the best thing was to give *her* a little nip, that maybe then she could relax sheself and she wouldn't feel so ashamed.

Johnny, we drank down *half* that decanter, and *still* Gregoria was too embarrassed to bend over and open up she cheeks. But at least the brandy had picked up she spirits a little bit, because one moment she was weeping big tears, and the next she let loose a string of giggles. Then I heard her start to humming a calypso – *pa-pum-pa-tee-tee pa-pum-pa-tee-tee* – that same tune everybody was singing that year. And Johnny, by this time *I*

158

was drunk as a jabmolassee too, because next thing you know we were both singing together, and then we were holding each other dancing right there in the kitchen just like this:

Since the Yankees arrived in Corpus Christi
All the younggirls frisky frisky!
They say the soldiers treat them nice
They give them a better price!

Sweet heart of Jesus! Johnny, you best help me to sit in the rocking chair again before I fall on the ground. What a thing eh, when you get old? Ninety-six years and Papa God *still* can't do me the kindness to kill off one time and finish! And after ten children I have these tot-tots hanging down between my knees almost to trip me. Sweet heart of Jesus! But Johnny, the wrinkles are not so bad. And the blood is not so yellow for an old-woman, and I could still wind up the bamsee a little bit, eh? *You* could wind up you bamsee a little bit youself, Johnny. Like you've got some of that rhythm in you blood too. *Ayeeyosmío!* What a thing is this life, eh?

So where I was now? Oh yes, so Gregoria and me were busy dancing, and singing, and so drunk with the brandy that we almost forgot this pin-cushion stuck inside she culo. Now I reminded her, and Gregoria said just one more little brandy, and she fired it back and tossed the glass over she shoulder shattering like one of those Greek weddings, and I fired a last one myself and tossed my *own* glass too. Now Gregoria slipped off she panties at last, she raised she skirts up around she waist. And something *very* peculiar, now she let loose a Tarzan cry like if she was Johnny Weissmuller heself swinging on he vine through the jungle,

Ow-ou ow-ou ow-ou waaah!

Now Gregoria bent over almost to touch she nose against the

159

flooring, and she spread she cheeks open with both hands as wide as they could go.

Johnny, it was like peering inside the deep dark hole of Calcutta. That was what I made the mistake to tell Gregoria, when straight away she started to curse me for insulting she coolie blood. I told her it wasn't that – and so far as I knew the only kind of blood she *didn't* have mixed up in she veins was coolie – the problem was that she bamsee was *so* black, and that kitchen so dark, I couldn't *see*. But maybe if she climbed up on top the counter a little closer to the light, and she knelt on all fours so that I could climb up on a chair behind her, maybe then I could get a better view from *above*? Gregoria seemed like she liked this idea good enough, and I gave her the decanter so she could take another swig, and I took another myself. Now I took up the bowl of pounded yams with butter to take out to the boys for they third plato, and I told Gregoria I would be right back with the chair. By this time of course the boys had finished they macaroni-pie, so I told them to please help theyselves to some pounded yams with butter. Of course, the boys were all a little bit concerned about Gregoria and me, and they wanted to know how were we progressing with the pin-cushion, and if I had managed yet to dissect it out? I told them that in truth we hadn't even located the precise position yet, but now we were going to try the *aerial reconnaissance* approach – which they could understand perfectly well since they were all soldiers theyselves – and I picked up the chair to carry it inside the kitchen.

By this time of course Gregoria had drunk down almost the entire decanter of brandy. But she said she'd saved a little bit for me, so I fired it back, and for some peculiar reason I tossed that expensive cut-crystal decanter shattering out the window. This, for some reason even *more* peculiar, sent us both into a fit of giggling like a pair of wicked schoolgirls behind the bush.

Now I went to give Gregoria a hand so she could climb up on top the chair and then the counter, but by this time we were both so drunk we could hardly stand – much less manage all this amount of climbing up on top chairs and counters and so on – and we ended up rolling on the floor together hugging each other, with me bouncing my head on the pipe beneath the sink. But it was as though we'd hit we funnybones instead of me near knocking myself unconscious, because this only sent us both into a fit of giggling again.

So it was five more minutes before Gregoria could manage to take she position kneeling on all fours up on top the counter – with her giggling and she blueblack bamsee standing tall in the air *jiggling* – and me ready in position standing on the chair behind her. Now I shoved with both my hands holding open she cheeks as wide as they could go. But even though she was closer now to the light, and even though *I* was bending over so close my nose was practically buried inside she culo – and Johnny, even though you might think I am only trying to make another one of my horrible metaphors, or *pums*, or whatever they call them – the truth is that I couldn't see a *fart*. On top of that I made the mistake to suggest to Gregoria that she raise up she right leg like if she was peeing on a lamppost, that maybe she culo could catch the light a little better, but this only sent her into a fit of cursing again. I told her I was only trying my best, and now I reminded her how much I loved her, *more* than if she was my own flesh and blood! Because just like always when I was drunk it made me not only a little bit more sentimental than usual, and melodramatic, but extra-sensitive also, and next thing you know *I* was weeping two big streams of tears rolling down my cheeks too. Sweet heart of Jesus! Now *Gregoria* began to feel bad, and she told me she felt very sorry for saying that Mummy, and she *even* lifted up she right leg high in the air just as I'd suggested! But Johnny, I still couldn't make out nothing

161

inside she black cavern of Calcutta a-tall. So I told Gregoria to hold she position right there a second, and I would be right back, that I was just going to fetch my firechief hat.

So I rushed past the boys hurrying down the stairs to the basement, and I took down my firechief hat from the nail where I had it hanging in case the Germans *did* arrive to bomb us just like the English promised, or for some other emergency like the one we had on we hands right now. You see, that hat was a special present one of my soldiers had given me only a few months previous, as he was in charge of the Fire Brigade at the Base. A big red fireman's hat shaped like a tall red barn, with the word CHIEF written in the tall capital letters across the front. But Johnny, the best feature of this hat was the special torchlight it had shining out the forehead, right out the middle of the *I*. So I lit up the torchlight and buckled the leather strap beneath my chin. But then I was thinking that even if I *did* manage to locate this pin-cushion stuck inside Gregoria's culo, I was going to need some kind of instrument to extract it out. Of course, right there hanging on the wall was those big pinchers which we used in the old days to carry blocks of ice when the ice-truck came – because that was long before they brought all these fancy Frigidaires from General Electric – that half the time you didn't have none long enough to freeze a block of ice *anyway*. But for some peculiar reason I never wanted to throw away those pinchers, and now I realized why, so I grabbed them down and took off running back to Gregoria. Of course, this time when I hurried past the diningroom with the torchlight shining out the forehead of my firechief hat, and these pinchers in my hands so big I could hardly carry them, the boys couldn't *help* but look up from they pounded yams with butter. They gave me another spontaneous chorus of '*Hot dog!*' and one of them came out with he joke of 'Make way for Mrs Frankenstein!' which sent them all to laughing again.

But that was not exactly the reaction Gregoria gave me. *She* let loose a cry of *serious* concern, this time like Johnny Weissmuller when he saw the Watusee-witchdoctor crouching in he doorway wearing he necklace of shrunken heads, the hatchet in one hand and the poison-tipped spear in the other:

Aye-aye-aye-aye-aye-aye!

Now she told me, 'No, no, Mummy! If you try to operate on me with them ice-pinchers it wouldn't be only the pin-cushion you pull out, it would be my whole asshole!'

Which is of course where we get the title for this story. But just as I told the boys, like all good titles it didn't have nothing whatsoever to do with the story itself, as it was only the enticement to make you want to hear it. Because Johnny, the truth is this story was *plenty* more serious than that, and it was *far* from finished. Because just as you would suspect Gregoria wouldn't let me nowhere near her with those ice-pinchers, less still to perform this operation. She didn't give me no choice but to pitch them out the window too, and then at last she let me approach her and climb up on top the chair. Now I could focus the torchlight of my firechief hat shining out the middle of my forehead – like the light blinking at the end of the dark tunnel of Gregoria's culo – just like that *other* famous story you *daddy* likes to tell of the physician who looked inside the asshole of he patient to find the eyeball looking out. But Johnny, maybe by this time that brandy had gone to my head in truth. Maybe that brandy had given me *double* vision, because this time it wasn't only one eyeball that I discovered inside Gregoria's culo looking back at me. This time it was *two*. Two little red eyes blinking curious at me from out the middle of a *living* pin-cushion, and the harder I looked the surer I became that's exactly what it was!

Now I outed the torchlight on my forehead like if I was ready to make some profound medical diagnosis, and I questioned Gregoria when was the last time she went swimming in the sea? Of course, she only looked at me all confused now with she head upside-down between she legs, and she told me, 'Only day-before-yesterday Mummy, when I went for a saltbath at Huevos Beach.' Well, I asked her, when was it you *first* happened to notice this particular pin-cushion? Day-before-yesterday Mummy, she answered, soon as I arrived back home from the beach. *Ah-ha!* I said, like if I'd already proved up everything clean clean. Now I told Gregoria to brace sheself, because this news I had for her wasn't so pretty a-tall. But at least she could dismiss any notions of that *dead-up* pin-cushion stuck inside she culo. 'Because day-before-yesterday,' I informed her, 'when you were busy enjoying you saltbath at Huevos Beach, when you weren't watching, a *porcupine-fish* mistook you bamsee for he own hole, and he swam up inside!'

Of course, Gregoria gave me a look now like if I wasn't only dead drunk, I was crazy out of my head too. But I only ignored her and told her not to worry sheself, that everything was under control, just to relax and put sheself completely in my hands. Because *I* had already thought up the idea how to get him out! I said to hold she position right there a second, and I would be right back. Now I took up the big bowl of coconut ice-cream that the boys could have for they dessert. I told them please to help theyselves, and I broke them the news of this porcupine-fish. Of course, boys being boys, all they were interested in for the moment was that coconut icecream, so I hurried back down to the basement because right there in the corner was the big pile of all you Uncle Reggie's fishing equipment. Rods and reels and nets and buckets and every kind of thing to do with this sport that you could imagine – but the only thing that interested *me* was that long pole with the big hook at the end – that same instrument they call a *fish-gaff*.

I was just starting up the stairs when I turned around again, and Johnny, I couldn't tell you what exactly I was thinking about, except maybe it had something to do with the brandy. Because now I slipped off my sandals to step with both feet inside those big tall rubber boots, reaching up as high as my *pussy*. And even though I couldn't hardly walk, and I almost tumbled backwards down the stairs, and every step I took the cuffs of those hard boots grated up uncomfortable against my pussy – not to mention the funny *squeaking* noise like walking in a pair of wet washykongs – even so those boys were so occupied with they dessert that they didn't even notice, which you could never believe until you taste Gregoria's coconut ice-cream.

She, of course, *did* notice. And after she gave me she Tarzan cry she told me, 'No, no, Mummy! If you try to operate on me with that fish-gaff it wouldn't be only my asshole you pull out, it would be my *tonsils* too!'

Sweet heart of Jesus! I didn't have no choice but to pelt that fish-gaff out the window. But for some peculiar reason I decided to do it like how those strongmen pelt they javelins in the Olympics. Of course, I could hardly even *walk* in those big tall rubber boots – less still to try to pelt javelin – and I ended up pelting *myself* flat on my face with my head bouncing against the castiron door of the oven. So it was a fortunate thing I was wearing my firechief hat, otherwise I would have knocked myself unconscious for the second time today! But by this time the boys had finished they dessert, and when they heard all this noise and commotion going on in the kitchen, they came running straight. Of course, Gregoria la Rosa was still kneeling there on the counter with she bamsee standing up tall in the air jiggling away, and she started to complain about being embarrassed again. But by this time I was back on my feet, and I explained to Gregoria how it was obvious that this problem, whatever it was, had grown beyond the proportions for we two to handle it alone. So the best thing was to ask the boys to take a look and offer they own opinions – that maybe they could help us decide if it was a pin-cushion, a sea-urchin or porcupine-fish or whatever else – and then they could advise us what we needed to do to get him out.

And that was exactly what happened. All the boys lined up behind Gregoria, and they took turns strapping on the firechief hat and climbing up on top the chair. One by one they took turns opening up Gregoria's cheeks to peer inside, one by one exclaiming they *oohs!* and *ahhs!* But it was the youngest soldier of all of them by the name of Billy Bud – that he happened at that particular time to be training as a field nurse – and he took only *one* look inside Gregoria before he let go a deep breath to tell us exactly what it was. He said it was a cyst the size of a *grapefruit* Gregoria had inside there, and we'd better get her to the hospital quick quick, because to him it looked like that cyst was ready to rupture any *second!*

Of course, Gregoria only let loose another whelp of pain. But I was already busy thinking, and I said that it was no use to call the *government* ambulance from the *government* hospital, because that ambulance wouldn't arrive before tomorrow morning. Then the doctor wouldn't get through he long line of patients stretching around the block to examine Gregoria before next *week* if she was lucky – that by then she culo will surely have exploded – and we will be picking up the pieces as far away as Sangre Grande. But Johnny, just as Gregoria let loose another whelp of pain, I got struck by the idea!

I told them we only option was to disguise Gregoria like if *she* was a soldier, and call the ambulance at the Base saying it was one of *you* boys who had this big emergency. Then they would come straight away with the siren bawling and the lights flashing, and they would take her straight to the hospital at the *Base*. So the only thing Gregoria had to do was to make good and sure she remained lying on she belly the whole time, and she didn't allow that doctor to see nothing more of her besides she dark bamsee, that if we were lucky he wouldn't even *realize* what was the particular sex of that culo he happened to be cutting open a-tall. 'Then,' I told them, 'the doctor will have this grapefruit out of Gregoria's backside quicker than you could pluck it off a tree!'

Of course, everybody liked this plan except Gregoria. But we all convinced her she didn't have no choice, and the boys took off running up the stairs to get her the uniform, with the cap and white gloves and boots and everything else. Johnny, by the time we finished painting on the sideburns and a fierce General Patton moustache, and we hung those tagdogs official around she neck, you couldn't tell her apart from *none* of them other soldiers.

Well everything worked perfect just as you would expect. So early the following morning we all went together to visit Gregoria in the recovery room of that hospital at the Base. Of course, by then they'd all realized she was a woman playing Carnival as a soldier – with those doctors laughing at the joke and making a big big pappyshow of Gregoria – and they even gave her a special ceremony to pin her with the purple heart! So I was sitting there beside her on the bed with all the soldiers gathered around, all of us like one big family as contented as we could be, and I reprimanded Gregoria saying that the *next* time she had a problem like this, *please* not to wait three days to tell us. 'Because the next time it wouldn't be only the grapefruit we find inside you culo, next time it would be a *watermelon!*' Now I waited for everybody to finish laughing, and I let loose a long sigh to express everybody's relief that at *last* this story had reached its satisfying end. 'Even though for poor Gregoria,' I told them, 'that probably wouldn't happen for another

167

week. And never mind what the doctor promised, *she* ending probably wouldn't be feeling too *happy* neither!'

So we were all sitting there around the table laughing, with the boys all congratulating me again saying how this was a good good story in truth, and one of them said, 'Yes, and it is a *moving* story too!' which sent us all to laughing again. And Johnny, that is the sure sure danger of telling stories. That sometimes it makes you lose sight of you own harsh reality you're living. Because all of a sudden we heard one set of bawling coming from inside the kitchen, so we took off running to find out what it was. And Johnny, that is the other problem about telling stories, that even when they *do* manage to help you see you own reality a little clearer, half the time it is in some way that is upside-down and it doesn't make no sense nor do no good for nobody a-tall. Because there in the kitchen was this Tanzanian Devil standing up on the chair before the counter, and he had poor Gregoria pinned on she belly across it with she bamsee standing up tall in the air. With this Tanzania wearing the shell of that *same* tattoo on he head like if he was trying to fulfil the fiction of *me* in my firechief hat – he pantaloons down around he knees with he nasty waterhose exposed – and he was fighting the fire with both hands, trying he best to shove the nozzle inside.

Sweet heart of Jesus! Before I could even think what might be the possible consequences, I pulled my pearlhandled pistol out from between my tot-tots again. I shoved it directly inside *he* bamsee-hole, and I closed my eyes to squeeze the trigger two times! Of course, all we heard was the soft metal *click click*. Because Johnny, as you know youself this was the little pistol made for me special by my great-uncle the General Francisco Monagas, when I was only a little girl, and it only had room in the chamber for two bullets, which of course I'd already shot off. I told Tanzania it was lucky for him I'd already exhausted all my ammunition, because this time for sure he'd be picking up the pieces of he culo all the way down under in he home of *Australia*.

Of course, the boys were all right there beside us, and they all loved Gregoria and me like if we were both mothers to them. So before you know the *biggest* one who was a boy called Godzilla grabbed hold of Tanzania's waterhose like if it was the handle of a tea kettle – and he with he pantaloons down around he knees stumbling he best to keep up – with Godzilla escorting him out the back door of the kitchen, around the house to the frontyard, for those boys could put one set of blows on him like pepper. I was there in the kitchen still consoling Gregoria after this big ordeal – and I even promised her I wouldn't tell that story of the pin-cushion no more – when the Colonel came begging on he knees please to call my boys off he partner, because they would murder him for sure. I told the Colonel he should have thought about that the *second* time he brought nastiness like this Tanzania inside the house, that he didn't have no manners nor respect for the people, and I would call my boys off but he must promise to pack up heself and he partner in they big white motorcar, and we don't never want to see they faces around here *never* again!

So that was that and now at least we could wipe we hands of them two for good. Of course, by this time it had already slipped my mind of that *other* scoundrel I had remaining still to contend with, because by then I was so exhausted it was all I could manage to drag myself up the stairs and tumble dead in the bed, like if we *had* lived through World War III in the house that evening in truth. Of course, who should I find there in my bed waiting for me but the King – and Johnny, I couldn't tell you what exactly *he* had in mind – all I can say is he was no longer even wearing he 'ceremonial gown'. *Ayeeyosmío!* Now I had to throw *him* out of the house too, and before I pelted he dirty old sheet behind him to slam the door and throw the bolt, I delivered him the same message that I gave the Kentucky Colonel!

So the next morning Gregoria and me were both there in the kitchen, both still half-asleep, still recovering weself after all this commess of the night before. But Johnny, it was as if we were still stuck in the same nightmare repeating itself all over again, because next thing we saw was you daddy coming with two dozen white roses that were so big he could hardly carry them, and he told us the King sent these for Gregoria and me. He said the *King* was waiting outside in he big white Cadillac motorcar, and he wanted to have a word of apology with the good madame. Johnny, you daddy had only reached to eleven or twelve years then just like you, and of course I reprimanded him straight away saying two things he *certainly* didn't inherit from me was neither my genes nor my genius for telling stories. Since of course he had he two characters confused one with the next, and the motorvehicles of they tales too. Because just as you know youself, it's the *Kentucky Colonel* who drives the big Cadillac motorcar, and the *King* who rides in he kickshaw. But now you daddy only got vex, and he told me he *did* know what the fuck he was talking about thank you very much – and if there was *any*body could cause more confusion and exasperation with she *ridiculous* stories it was you, Mummy – so why don't you go back with the Warrahoons in the bush in Venezuela where you came from, since you never even learned to speak *English* proper! And now you daddy said that if we didn't believe him, we could go to the front door and see for weself.

Johnny, just as you daddy described there was the King sitting in the back seat of the big Cadillac motorcar smoking he cigar, with the Kentucky Colonel sitting behind the wheel just as usual, he partner Tanzania beside him. So all I could think was that this King and the Colonel must have reconciled theyselves and made friends overnight – because only the evening before they were at each other's throats like Mussolini and Eisenhower in truth – and I was so *pleased* to see this thing I couldn't help myself from running out the house to thank them! And maybe with my hangover I still had a little bit of that sentimentality left over swimming in my veins too, because now I said that to see the two of them happy and peaceful together like brothers had filled my heart with hope for the world. That maybe one day we *could* learn to love eachother like human beings again, and we could put an end at last to this terrible terrible war! But the King only raised he hand slow in the air for me to shut my mouth, he took he big cigar out from between he teeth, and he told me he was very sorry to be the one to bust my bubble. 'But before you say another word, my good Madame, let me inform you of the true nature and beauty of this and *all* friendships between men and nations alike. Because the fact is that I have bought out the Colonel here lock, stock, and all he barrels too.'

The King went on to explain how *he* was now the proud owner of the entire Kentucky Fried Empire worldwide. And at this precise moment while we occupied weselves with smalltalk, he workers and baboo-boys were busy not only writing over the names on all the signs, but they were painting over the portrait of the Colonel here with another of yours truly, on every one of them pasteboard barrels! And Johnny, to prove he point he took up the bucket-shaped container on the seat there beside him, he turned it around to show me the picture like a mirror-reflection of he *own* fat face smiling out the front – complete with the tall white turban, and the ruby upon he forehead flashing, and the long grey beard – and he told me please to help myself to a drumstick of

King of Chacachacari Fried!

Oui fute, papa-yo! I was so vex to see this thing now I was spitting *fire*. I asked the King if he didn't realize that Colonel Sanders was a household name not only in every proud home in America, but in every falling-down tin shanty, and mudhut, and rotting little wood-shack in the whole of the Caribbean too? That *Colonel Sanders* was the name we all grew up on. And *Colonel Sanders* was the name we learned to identify weself with. And you just can't take him away from us no more than you could wake up one morning out of the blue and announce to the world that the Queen Mother is henceforth going to be called the *Dairy* Queen! On top of that, who the ass ever heard of nothing more ridiculous and infuriating than King of Chacachacari Fried Chicken, that you couldn't even *pronounce* it proper without tripping over you own tongue and falling flat on top you face!

Well! the King realized he had touched some tender and unexpected place in me in truth. Because he changed he tune straight away. Now he said that even though it was never sound negotiations tactics to mix up one set of business transactions with another, in fact the governments did it all the time. So maybe if we *could* manage to come to some kind of agreement, he could throw in a special clause at the bottom of the page in fine print, and he could change back the names of all the restaurants to *Kentucky* Fried, with the Colonel's face again smiling out from all he barrels. 'Because come to think of it just as you said youself, good Madame, King of Chacachacari Fried *is* a little bit cumbersome on the tongue in truth. On top of that he workers are having a very difficult time squeezing in all those letters around the circumference of the pasteboard barrels, and every five minutes one of those exasperating illiterate little baboos comes molesting me again in they infuriating sing-song coolie-voices, "Is it four *c*s and three *h*s in that *Chacachacari* Daddy, or the other way around?"'

I told the King that after all that confusion of him naked in my bed last night, and that Tanzania trying to take advantage of poor Gregoria, I wasn't so much inclined to welcome them back inside the house a-tall. And I didn't know what kind of 'agreement' he was talking about – that straight away it made me suspicious – but if that is what I have to do to protect we heritage, then that is what I have to do. 'But maybe this time,' I told him, 'we can have a quiet discussion friendly and civilized without no bub-ball about it for a change, and Gregoria la Rosa could serve us a coffee, or some other nice little refreshment.'

But Johnny, I don't know why I said that about Gregoria except to repeat something I'd heard in this nightmare someplace before – and I only put goatmouth *loud* on myself saying it too – because when I turned around to look for Gregoria, there she was posing like a jamette up against the Cadillac on Tanzania's side! With the two of them making eyes together, and Gregoria batting she lashes for him like a battimamselle – as if they'd *already* stirred back they old flame from the *last* time he and Kentucky came inside the house trying to bamboozle us with they swindle of the pizza parlour – but that of course is another story. And now I took a moment to study this Tanzania with he smooth bronze skin, and hair, and he ice-blue shining eyes – and I remembered how much of a *handsome* devil he was in truth – and once again I realized how Gregoria and me were *both* in hot water with these men up over we heads.

Sweet heart of Jesus! I didn't have *no* choice now but to invite them all back inside the house, even though I knew better. So everybody took they seats again in the parlour, and Gregoria whispered to Tanzania how she was just disappearing in the kitchen a moment to warm up she demitasse, and I told her in that case please make my own a *double*. And Johnny, we'd scarce even had a chance to sit down when I began to notice a little hand reaching out from behind the couch where the King was sitting, and then a *next* little hand reaching out from the next side of the couch behind the Colonel. All in a sudden you daddy and you Uncle Amadao jumped up together to take off running out the door bawling,

'Fakees fakees pudinum bakees!'

and I had to call them back and reprimand them both please to return to the gentlemen they moustaches and Father Christmas beard. The *former* to the Kentucky Colonel and the *latter* to the King. Of course, you know you daddy and you uncle as good as me, that whatever I tell them they are going to do exactly the opposite. And Johnny, that cabrón King and the pendejo Colonel wasn't no better! Because when I looked again it was the *King* wearing those catfish moustaches and the *Colonel* the Father Christmas beard – like if it wasn't bad enough they had to take advantage of us boldface so – they wouldn't even do us the courtesy of keeping up they attempts to disguise it!

Gregoria came back with the coffees now and she passed them around, and I heard her whisper to Tanzania that she thought maybe she'd heated up she demitasse a little bit *too* hot, and could he do her the kindness please of blowing some cool air on it. *Papa-yo!* Two of them were sitting there in the corner giggling together, with me already beginning to feel nervous, when I turned to the King to ask him what did he have in mind for this 'agreement'. But now it was the *Colonel* who answered me instead of the King – with him sitting there stroking he Father Christmas beard like he'd been doing it all he life, instead of only for two minutes – so now I was beginning to feel not only nervous but *confused* too. The Colonel told me, 'Skip, before we fire up the peacepipe, I got a little something here in my piggy might be of interest to you!' With that he put on the coffeetable he red metal strongbox that used to have he *own* pic-

174

ture painted on the lid – except now of course it had the portrait of that King which was logical enough – and he turned the little key in the lock to open it up. Now he took out ten stacks of Yankee money that were so fat I didn't know how he squeezed the rubberbands around them without bursting, and he piled them up careful in front of me, reaching up as tall as my own narices. *Papa-yo!* The Colonel knew good enough how nervous it made me to see all that amount of money, and worse still if I had to *smell* it too – worse than a starving Warrahoon catching the scent of a barbecued quenk – so now I was not only nervous and confused, I was a little bit distracted on top.

Johnny, by now you know this Colonel as good as anybody else, that he didn't like nothing better than to hear heself talk, and most of the time it wasn't nothing more than *nonsense*. Because the first thing he gave me was one big long palaver about what were the precise reasons he'd grown out he Father Christmas beard. He told me that it was the finishing touches for he new career as the 'famous American radio-personality'. He said how he had been waiting he whole life for somebody like the King here to bail him out of the fried chicken business – that he was so sick of looking at frenchfries and fried chicken all day, every day, morning noon and night, he was beginning to feel like if *he'd* been rolled in the special batter and deep-fried in a vat of three-day-old grease heself – that the only thing that business was good for was making youself a fortune. And the proof, he said, was stacked up right here beneath you own sniffer. But all that belonged to the past, he said. All that belonged to some *other* invented character of advertising *genius*, which he had already discarded in less time than it took to think him up. 'Because Skip,' he told me, 'what I truly am in my heart of hearts is a *Houdini* of the higher frequencies. A thoroughbred, Triple Crown, Kentucky Derby *deee-jay!* That is to say, Skip, an *artiste* of the airwaves!'

Johnny, already I was beginning to feel a little bit dizzy with all the Colonel's talk, with my ears already ringing, and I told him that first of all, I didn't know what the ass a Father Christmas beard had to do with being a disk-jockey. 'Because we are talking about radio here and not television that that machine hasn't even been invented yet, thank the lord, for us to have to look at you fat face on the screen on *top* of hearing the endless flapping of you trap too! Second of all,' I told him, 'please come to the point and tell us *who* the ass is this famous American radio-personality he was talking about, and no more diarrhoea of the mouth like if you've eaten parrot and it has upset you stomach.' So now the Colonel finished the last sip of he demitasse, he put down the little cup delicate to rise to he feet, and he announced for all of us sitting there that henceforth, he would appreciate for us to call him by he new namenick of

Wolfman Jack

Sweet heart of Jesus! Johnny, I gave him the same monkeyface you are giving *me* right now, and I told him if he thinks I was born yesterday and I was foolish enough to swallow *that* one he had another thing coming. Because that was the most blatant, ridiculous, *upsetting* anachronism or whatever the fuck they called it that I had ever heard in all my life! 'Because the real life Wolfman Jack probably isn't even *born* yet, and even if he is, everybody with sense knows he won't be appearing on the radio with he big caveman beard for another *twenty* years!'

Of course, the Colonel didn't even answer me because he didn't *have* an answer to give me, and he only changed the subject. He went on to explain how he had made a very careful study of the whole island, and the best location for this radio station was right upstairs in the garret of this very house. Because the important thing was to locate *we* transmission antenna far enough away from all that big set of communica-

176

tions Eiffel Towers they had at the Base, otherwise all the signals would get all confused one with the next. The other important thing was that this roof was among the tallest of all the houses, with the big empty garret beneath to put in all the equipment – and the soundproof glass booth for the DJ with the microphone, the record player and switchboard and all the rest – and the special red light above that said '*On the air!*'.

Well! I interrupted the Colonel first thing to tell him how that was all very nice, but then *he* interrupted *me* straight away and he said please to call him *Jack*. So I started again and I told this *Jack* how that was all very nice, and I was pleased for he new career that I couldn't think of nothing more appropriate myself, and if he wanted to pay me all this pile of Yankee money only to put the lightning rod for the antenna on the roof, and the microphone and record player in the garret, then I didn't even need a moment to consider it, 'so let's just jump in you Cadillac right now and go straight to the bank for me to make the deposit!'

Of course, now that the conversation turned to the part about *money*, this Colonel or Kentucky or Wolfman or whoever the ass he was started singing a different tune. He said once again how he had made a careful study for this radio station, and he'd priced all the equipment that we would require down to the last dead Indian nickel, and how these ten-thousand dollars here on the table represented exactly *half* the requisite funds. 'But,' he said, 'we will certainly recover these initial, *in*significant expenditures and *plenty* more besides in no time a-tall. Because I don't have to tell you that radio stations make they fortunes selling *advertisements*. And Skip, there ain't *no*body knows *that* business better than me! As a matter of fact,' he said, 'I have already bespoken you good friend the Sergeant Warren at the Base, and the American Army is already mobilized to announce all they endless Uncle Sam

177

propaganda exclusively on *we* radio station. In addition,' he told me, 'the King here will be paying us through he gold teeth for *you* to sing he Chacachacari chicken-jingle over the air every fifteen minutes.' But Johnny, when I looked over at the King for him to verify all this he was only snoring out loud, and worse even than that, now I noticed that not only had he switched he Father Christmas beard for the handlebar-moustaches, he'd stuck them on upside-down.

So just when I was telling myself that all this radio station business wasn't nothing more than another big swindle, this Jack or whoever he was jumped to he feet all excited again. 'Skip,' he said, 'now comes the sweetest part of this partnership. The *romantic* part! Because everybody sitting here knows there's only *one* person in the world who has defined the fine art of farting out the *polite* orifice better than me. And this particular person,' he told us, 'happens to be my *backup* DJ. My right-hand-woman. Think of her as *Fanny Fox*. Think of her as *Jackal Jill*, *Kitty Coyote*, or whichever namenick you choose. But Skip', he said now with he face as purple as a governor plum, '*I* like to think of her as my own little *Lady Lobo!*'

Sweet heart of Jesus! I told this Jack please not to send poor old Mrs Carmichael rolling with laughter in she grave. 'Because everybody in the world knows you are the biggest *buller* ever to embarrass the entire American Army. So don't play the ass with me talking no romance, unless you want to tell me about somebody else with a *different* set of cooking utensils.' Furthermore, I told him, ten-thousand dollars was all I had in the world, that my husband Barto had left me that money expressly to send the boys to study medicine in Canada when they grew up. And even that money would have finished a long time ago, if the good Sergeant Warren at the Base hadn't come to me one day out of the blue, and he handed me over another ten-thousand only to make this boarding house for the soldiers. 'So even though that dream of the famous Lady Lobo on the radio *does* sound to me a little bit appealing, I don't have no illusions about what is my small and *insignificant* place in this world. It is to raise children. And now that I have dedicated my whole life to caring for them, and worrying over them day and night, and I am almost finished at last with only two remaining, now I have to start all over again with my boarding house full of all you young American boys.'

'*Ah!*' said this Jack jumping to he feet again like he had ants in he pants. 'But every soldier sitting here knows well enough you *do* have another secret dream personality. Another fantasy life. Not only in you heart of hearts, but first thing every morning in the *shower* before the rest of us can even get chance to open we eyes. Because every excruciating morning of life we *all* have the same simultaneous nightmare of you as the famous Italian Opera Prima Donna! And of course,' said this Jack, 'let me remind you of the other important feature of this radio station – in addition to the canned music, the news briefs and all the rest – which will be the continuous *live* appearance as much as you heart desires of local *singing* talent!'

Johnny, I informed this jackass of a Colonel once again that he didn't know a fart what he was taking about. Because the only reason for that hideous opera every morning at the top of my lungs was because it was the only way foolproof to get all *you* lazy backsides out of bed and down the stairs to breakfast. Because the truth is that I don't even know how to *speak* Italian, less still to try to sing it. And even though I can't speak English too good neither, that is the language I love best to sing. 'So listen here Jack,' I told him, 'let me inform you of one more thing. In *my* heart of hearts I am nothing but pure West Indian. And if I *do* have a secret fantasy dream of becoming the famous singer on the radio – day and night as much as my heart desires like the one that you have just mentioned – it is *only* as the world's first female *Calypsonian!'*

So that was that and just as you have already guessed we all piled directly in the Cadillac to go straight to the bank – all except for Gregoria and that Tanzania, because I didn't even want to *think* where they'd disappeared to – and I took out the ten-thousand dollars. Of course, before I handed it over I reminded the King about changing back the names of all the restaurants. The King said not only that, in addition he'd like to invite us all to a celebratory lunch to toast we new partnership. I said fine, but only if he took us to *Kentucky* Fried. And when lunch was finished they dropped me home, that by this time of course Tanzania was sitting on the front stoop waiting for us, the big smile on he face. So he jumped in the front seat beside Jack for the three of them to take off again. They said how they would be back in no time with all the radio equipment, and I stood there in the street watching the three of them and all that money disappearing around the corner behind a cloud of dust. So what to do? Only thing was to go *straight* to the kitchen to have a good long talk with Gregoria about this Tanzania.

Of course, instead of me reprimanding Gregoria, she was the one to reprimand *me*, and she said she couldn't believe she had such a foolish and ignorant woman for she own mother. Because didn't I realize those three weren't nothing more than crooks, and swindlers, and how could I *possibly* hand them over all that amount of money for some cock-and-bull story of this Wolfman Jack and he Lady Lobo on the radio? I told her now was a fine time to come criticizing, and why wasn't she there to advise me proper instead of disappearing with that Tanzanian Devil when I needed her most, and I told her *she* would be the first one fighting us down to sing a calypso as soon as the light came on that said *'On the air!'*. Gregoria said we would be lucky enough ever to see those wadjanks again – now that they had all the money – never mind singing about it. But just as she was saying this a big smile burst across she face – that same smile we are all familiar with of the younggirl with the spider crawling inside she panties – and now she told me, 'Well, if they do happen to show up tonight, *one* of them wouldn't be leaving so hurry hurry again. Because *this* time I am going to fix him up good with a little stay-home!'

Sweet heart of Jesus! I wasn't even sure what this *stay-home* was all about, but I knew from the sound of Gregoria's voice that it was something I didn't *want* to know nothing much about neither. She said the first thing she had to do was to go in the bush to pick some green *caraili* – that was a bitter bitter kind of fruit shaped like a bumpy cucumber, that sometimes we called it *womb*-fruit – and then she could boil this caraili in a tea and take some, and that would bring on she menses. And Johnny, sure enough hardly had Gregoria returned from the bush for her to make this tea and drink down some, when she menses started to flow. Next she boiled up a big pot of rice, she put it to drain in the sink, and then Gregoria rested the colander of rice on the floor in the corner of the kitchen. Now she slipped off she panties, she raised she skirts up a little bit, and she spent the next half-hour squatting down over that rice, the big smile on she face!

I told her if she gave Tanzania this rice to eat with that *nastiness* mixed up inside it, surely he would taste something *funny*. But Gregoria only continued smiling, and she said she was going to disguise it by cooking up the rice in a big pelau – with stewed chicken, pigeonpeas, raisins and plenty pepper – one special bowl with the stay-home for him, and a next big bowl of pelau *without* it for everybody else. And Johnny, Gregoria had scarce finished cooking these two big pots of pelau for us to take for the dinner, when the next thing we heard was the horn *bee-beep! bee-beep! bee-beep!* blowing in front the house.

So we took off running to greet the King and Jack in they Cadillac motorcar – and following behind them of course was the big camouflaged jitney of the US Army loaded down with all the equipment – and Tanzania behind the wheel. He spent the next three hours off-loading all this amount of radio machines from out the jitney. With Jack giving the orders and talking a mile a minute as usual, Tanzania sweating and struggling to tote all these big machines up inside the garret. On top of that I made him carry upstairs all my old calypso records, and Tanzania almost fell off the roof and busted he head trying to erect the tall lightning rod-antenna. Now Jack announced for everybody to assemble upstairs in the garret, and he pointed out to us there in the corner half-hidden behind all this amount of big machines blinking away, the special soundproof glass booth for the DJ! Of course, it had the record player with all my tall stack of calypso records just beside, the fancy microphone shaped like a miniature planet Saturn with the rings going around it there on the table, and sure enough right above we heads was the special red light that said '*On the air!*'.

Now Jack went inside the booth, and he locked the door behind him to take he seat at the DJ table. He switched on the big microphone, he lit up the red light above he head that said '*On the air!*', and now Jack began to talk. Of course, we couldn't hear not a word he was saying inside that soundproof glass box, like a fat goldfish inside he bowl only moving he jaws blowing bubbles. So we all took off running down the stairs to the parlour, with Gregoria and Tanzania and me gathered around the old crackling ElectroDelux, the King tuning the dial. And Johnny, sure enough when he found the station, the voice that came booming out was the same familiar one of Jack heself! Of course, it wasn't no less *nauseating* coming from that old Delux as in real life neither, but now at least you had the special advantage of being able to shut him off. And that was just what I was preparing to do when we heard Jack announce, 'And don't forget folks to listen in at nineteen- hundred hours tonight for the inaugural broadcast of the *Lady Lobo Calypso Show!* featuring – you guessed it ladies and gentlemen – the one and only *deeee*-jay Lady Lobo! And tonight we own Lady Lobo will be introducing a very special guest for she inaugural performance, none other than the world's first female calypsonian – you guessed it ladies and gentlemen – the one and only *Lady Lobo!*' So everybody hugged me up and congratulated me clapping they hands on my back, even though this Jack made me sound like a crazy person with three different personalities, and I switched him off because by now the boys had arrived hungry from the Base, and the rest of us were famished too.

All except for me. Because Johnny, *I* was so excited and nervous about singing my calypsos over the air tonight, that I lost all my appetite. On top of that I was a little bit distracted, because when Gregoria brought in the two big bowls of pelau and she put them down on the table for me to serve them around – and she gave me a mischievous wink and a nod of she nose to remind me which bowl was which – even so I made the fatal mistake of confusing one with the next. *Well!* those soldiers tasted only a little taste of this pelau, and they said it is the *best* Gregoria had ever cooked. The King said the same, and when they all started to eat, it was like if they would never finish! They *ate ate ate* – only pausing long enough to bawl out 'Please pass some more of that delicious pelau!' – and then they ate some more. Johnny, they ate like if they were blind. They ate like if there was no tomorrow. They ate like if a starving jab-jab had jumped inside they skins, because they just couldn't get enough of this pelau. All except for me and that Tanzania. Because in truth, we were the only two sitting there at the table

183

who *didn't* get a good dose of Gregoria's stay-home. Even though we wouldn't realize my mistake nor see the full *results* of it before another hour.

Because now it was time for the *Lady Lobo Calypso Show!* Of course, the King and the boys all said they wouldn't miss it for nothing in the world, and they dragged theyselves groaning out to the parlour. All except for Tanzania, because Gregoria held him back saying she was very sorry but *they* had other plans for tonight, starting with a little after dinner demitasse. But I didn't even have time to worry about Gregoria none, because I took off straight up the stairs inside the garret. As soon as Jack saw me he opened the glass door for me to come inside the soundproof booth for the DJ, I took my seat there on the chair beside him, and he announced, 'Ladies and gentlemen, we will now have a one minute test for the Emergency Broadcast System.' He turned off the big microphone and the red light above we heads, and he explained to me the switchboard and all the gadgets he had there on the table. He told me not to pay no attention to him and the King working on all those *other* big machines outside – that they job was to make sure the signal was transmitting strong and clear – and *my* job was only to keep on announcing and singing continuous without a pause just as loud as I could manage. Unless, of course, I was spinning a disk, in which case I must make sure to play it with the volume turned to the max, and in that way every last one of my listeners even to the farthest corners of the Caribbean could hear me. 'One last thing,' he told me. 'Don't forget every two minutes to remind everybody that *Uncle Sam wants you!* and the *Colonel has you fried chicken too!* because every time you repeat those jingles it's as easy as cash ringing in the register!'

Johnny, next thing you know Jack lit up the special red light again that said '*On the air!*', he switched on the big fancy Saturn-shaped microphone, and he locked the door behind him. *Oui fute, papa-yo!* All I could think was to announce to everybody that they were listening to *The Lady Lobo Calypso Show!* and how the Lady Lobo sheself would be singing them a few hot calypsos later on in the programme, 'but first let me play you a tune that is one of my favourites, and you will all recognize the universal theme, by none other than the Roaring Lion':

> *Miss Dorothy went to the river to bathe*
> *And Mr Catfish made a raid!*
> *She started to wiggle*
> *She started to giggle*
> *Miss Dorothy bawled, 'Oh my! Oh me!'*
> *'Look, Mr Catfish is nibbing me pussy!'*

Johnny, truth is that after the second chorus I couldn't *help* myself but sing along with Lion, and when the record was finished I couldn't help but sing them the chorus a couple more times all by myself! I sang it as loud as I could manage, just like Jack told me. After that of course I didn't want to play no more records, and I announced to everybody that the Lady Lobo would now give them she *own* rendition of a tune by the Lord Invader, and of course everybody will recognize this one:

> *Rum and coca-cola*
> *Down to Point Cumana!*
> *Mothers and they daughters*
> *Working for the Yankee dollar!*

When I finished with that one I sang them a golden oldie from the Lord Executor. I sang them a tune from Pretender. And just as I had started in on the next calypso from the Mighty Growler, I looked up to see Gregoria pounding on the glass door of that DJ booth, she face all sweaty and puffed up like a pomseetay. But before I could even have a chance to unlock the door she took off running again – and Johnny, now the strangest thing – instead of that *Tanzania* chasing behind her just as you would expect, it was three of those young American soldiers. And following behind trying he best to keep up was the old King heself. *Well!* I could only think that this was very very peculiar in truth – that maybe those boys were hungry for some more pelau? – but I didn't even have time to consider it much as already I'd finished singing the Growler calypso, and I'd just started in on a next one by Atilla the Hun. But before I could even reach the chorus Gregoria came pounding on the glass door of the booth again. Once again I didn't even get a chance to open up before she took off running for the second time, and now it was *five* of those soldiers chasing behind her *plus* the King. But I hardly paid them no mind, because now I was singing a new tune by El Tigre that was one of my favourites.

Next thing Gregoria came pounding again, and when at last I opened the door she slammed it back shut and locked it behind her first thing, and she scrambled beneath the table! So of course I finished the El Tigre tune after the next verse, I announced to everybody that we would now have a three minute test for the Emergency Broadcast System, and I switched off the microphone and crawled down under the table too. Now I asked Gregoria to please explain what was going on, and why was she interrupting me pounding down the door of my DJ booth every five minutes, that she couldn't even wait for my Lady Lobo programme to finish? Gregoria told me *I* was the one who needed to do the explaining. Because when she put those two bowls of pelau on the table I must have confused them one with the next, and I must have served that stay-home to everybody *except* Tanzania. Because how else could *he* be the one snoring away dead in the bed, with all of those *soldiers* bazodee all in a sudden chasing her all over the house, and the King, that the only place she could find safe to escape them was right here inside this DJ box!

But before I could have a chance to understand what Gregoria was trying to tell me, the soldiers had already sniffed her out hiding beneath the table, and now *they* were the ones pounding down the door and all the glass walls of this DJ booth. Of course, this booth was made from heavy heavy soundproof glass with the door locked-up tight, so there wasn't *no* way for those soldiers to get at her. And Johnny, that was a good thing too, because in no time a-tall those boys turned into a school of woman-eating sharks swimming around the bait in a feeding *frenzy*. With the bait of course we own beloved Gregoria la Rosa! Next thing one of the soldiers decided he could *never* hold heself back – he folded out he ventral flipper and began vigorous to back-stroking it up and down – and soon enough the remainder of those man-sharks were doing just the same! Johnny, it was like drowning beneath the white-caps! Like being swallowed up in a sea-froth of foaming waves! Because not until each *one* of those boys and the old Kingfish too had relieved theyselves three and four different times – with the whole of this glass cage dripping now with they fishy white fertilizer – could they turn they backs on Gregoria and carry theyselves all drained-out straight downstairs to they beds.

Well! after a time Gregoria and me crawled out cautious from beneath the table, and we looked around with we mouths wide open gaga in truth. Because Johnny, it was like staring up at the overturned glass bowl of the night sky, washed one horizon to the next with the milky way! Of course, Gregoria was still plenty vex with me over all this stay-home confusion. I told her instead of cursing me, she should thank Papa God for letting her escape those soldiers with she life, not to mention she little pussy still safe between she legs instead of torn to shreds too. That the *next* time she planned to experiment with this stay-home please to give me ample warning, that I could call in the National Guard first! I said that the only thing for us to do now was try to enjoy weself singing a few calypsos. Because in truth, this Emergency Test had been going for a good half-hour!

So I switched on the microphone and announced to everybody that I had just been joined in the studio by the world's only *other* female Calypsonian – nobody but *Mistress Matilda the Man-Eater* sheself – and we would now like to give you we own *duet*-rendition of a little Roaring Lion, since I knew this one was a calypso Gregoria could never resist:

> *Pompous was Mistress Matilda*
> *And haughty she was so lovely!*
> *Sagaboys tried to no avail*
> *Bigshots tried and they too failed!*
> *Even a Yankee soldier, unbuckled he holster*
> *She said, 'Boy, careful playing with you hand grenade!'*

Johnny, when we finished with that tune Gregoria and me gave them a little Growler. We gave them some Atilla the Hun. Gregoria and me gave them a calypso from Lord Executor, and Lord Invader, Lord Pretender and every *other* Lord we could think of, and then we gave them some more. We sang them as loud as we could, just like Jack said. We sang until we were hoarse, and blue in the face, and we just couldn't sing another calypso. Not until *three* o'clock did Gregoria and me sing them *both* we national anthems of 'God Save We Queen' and 'We Star-Spangled Banner', we signed off reminding them that *Uncle Sam wants you and the Colonel has you fried chicken too!* and we wished everybody a very exhausted good night.

Of course, Gregoria and me slept till three o'clock the following afternoon too. Both we voices so raw we couldn't speak a word before we took a cup each of my secret medicine, a little hot water with a teaspoon of honey, a dash of Angostura bitters, and a stiff shot of brandy. At last Gregoria sucked she teeth, and she said she wouldn't be surprised if those three wadjanks hadn't cleared out from the house over night with all they fancy equipment. That maybe that would be the *best* thing, so we wouldn't have to deal with them nor they radio station again. I said well, there was one quick way to find out, and I led her inside the parlour and flipped on the old ElectroDelux. Of course, I flipped it off straight away again, because the voice that came booming out above the crackling was the familiar nauseating one of Jack heself. So Gregoria and me took a deep breath, we braced weself, and we climbed the stairs inside the garret. When we looked in the corner there was Tanzania with a clothespin pinching he nose, and he had on some elbow-length rubber gloves, wiping off the last of that fish fertilizer from the glass door of that DJ booth. Of course, shining above he head was the special red light that said *'On the air!'*, but there wasn't no *Jack* inside the box dee-jaying a-tall.

Just as I was beginning to think how this was very peculiar, who should stick he head out from between two of those big machines blinking away beside us but the King, and he took off the headphones he had clamping around he ears. He congratulated us saying what a great success we Calypso Show was last night – that people had been calling in all morning to find out who was that Lady Lobo and Mistress Matilda? and could they please send us full-length photos? and when were they going to make they first album? – and the callers all said how they couldn't *wait* to hear Lady Lobo and Mistress Matilda singing together on they radio programme again tonight! I told the King I was very sorry but the show was *cancelled* until further

189

notice. Because Gregoria and me had strained we voices so bad last night we would be lucky if we ever sang a calypso again! And in truth, all this radio business was beginning to smell a little bit like toe-jam to me too, so please tell me how the fuck that Jack was *not* dee-jaying inside the booth, but even so he voice continued booming as exasperating as ever out the old Delux?

The King smiled and explained how Jack was taking a little nap downstairs in he room after he morning broadcast. Because just the *opposite* of what Gregoria was wishing that maybe the three of them could have cleared out from the house over night – in fact they'd all three *moved in* to take up permanent residence – which was only appropriate, the King informed us, since we were all now partners together in the radio station. He went on to explain that the reason there was nobody dee-jaying inside the booth was because now it was time for the *Local News Programme*, so of course Jack left the same loop-tape playing again like he did every afternoon. 'Because just as you know youself, good Madame, there ain't no such thing as *news* in this Caribbean. And even if there *was* some new hot political scandal and corruption in the government, you couldn't scarcely distinguish it from the other hot political scandal and government corruption of the day before.' *Well!* I told this pendejo King that on the one hand, what he was saying was partly true. But on the other hand, I was *not* so pleased to hear that the three of them had moved in to take up permanent residence with us. But I didn't even have time to consider it much, because Gregoria and me had better get weself cooking straight away, if we planned to have the dinner prepared for everybody by tonight.

Of course, before we could even taste that coconut pudding Gregoria and me had prepared for dessert, we took off running up the stairs to the garret. Because now it was time for the *Lady Lobo and Mistress Matilda Calypso Show!* Johnny, not before the sun began to rise at *six* o'clock the following morning, did Gregoria and me sing them we national anthems to sign off at last from off the air. We slept until four o'clock the following afternoon, and when we finished taking we daily medicine Gregoria and me climbed the stairs to the garret, and we begged the King please to send Tanzania to pick up a couple barrels, because we were just too exhausted to try to cook the dinner! The King said that would be very fine, just as it should be. That it was he great privilege to treat the famous Lady Lobo and Mistress Matilda to a few barrels of he chicken, and the only important thing was to rest up you voices for you calypso programme tonight! So soon enough that became part of the regular routine too. Gregoria and me singing on the radio till five or six every morning, sleeping till four or five in the afternoon, and Tanzania going every evening to pick up the dinner.

But then one evening Gregoria and me decided to go along with Tanzania to pick up the fried chicken in the Cadillac motorcar. That maybe a little outing in the fresh air with the top down would do us some good, because we hadn't left the house in more than two weeks since we radio station went on the air. So I was sitting in the front seat beside Tanzania, Gregoria standing on the seat behind us waving to everybody – because this sudden fame of Mistress Matilda had gone a little bit to she head in truth – when I decided to flip through the stations on that radio in the dash. Of course, the *last* person in the world I wanted to listen to was Jack, and even though I was trying my hardest to skip over the station, what I couldn't understand was how I managed to do it so *easy*. Now I changed my mind turning the dial slowly in the opposite direction – trying this time to tune Jack in – but I couldn't find him *a-tall*.

So I was thinking this was a little bit peculiar, but I didn't mention it to nobody, and when we reached back home I went to the parlour to check the old ElectroDelux. Johnny, the funny thing *now* was that no matter *which* station I tuned the dial to, I heard the same nauseating voice of Jack in he same old loop-tape that we had all memorize by heart by now, on every single station! The other funny thing I noticed was a red wire sticking out from the back of this old radio, in addition to the plug, that I was *sure* I'd never seen this red wire before. Of course, I went down on my hands and knees straight away to trace it out, and I followed it beneath the rug, behind the couch, around the desk and the rocking chair and out through the window. Now I climbed up on top the rocking chair and stuck my head out the window, trying my best to see where was this wire connected. But no matter *how* far I stretched myself I couldn't see it a-tall, and I gave the wire a little tug. Now I was starting to get vex, and I gave the wire a tug again. Of course, that rocking chair wasn't the most stable of footings neither, and next thing you know I was tumbling out the window flat on top my face – and just as I was spitting out a big mouthful of dirt – a heavy metal object came *ka-plonk!* down on top my head, near knocking me flat unconscious.

So when I recovered myself from this blow a few minutes later, and my eyeballs centred in they sockets for me to examine what this red wire that I was still clutching tight in both my fists was connected to – Johnny, instead of finding that big lightning rod-antenna like you were expecting – it was only that same fancy Saturn-shaped microphone from inside the DJ booth! How I could've pulled it out from that sealed-off glass box I didn't have the least idea – unless Jack had forgotten the glass door open – but the one thing I knew now for sure, was that the *only* radio we'd been broadcasting to all this time was only we *own* old Elec-troDelux inside the parlour. So Johnny, now I began to think!

And just as fortune would have *already* had it, Kentucky happened to be running a special promotion that very evening of they homestyle BBQ Baked Beans. Not only that, but Gregoria and me were so *sick* of eating fried chicken every night, that we told Tanzania we could *never* satisfy weself with only a couple servings of they simple side. Because we wouldn't settle for *nothing* less than two of they jumbo-sized pasteboard *tubs*, one for Gregoria and one for me.

Johnny, when the time came for dinner we ate them down too! And no matter how much those soldiers begged us for some, we wouldn't give them even a taste. So as soon as Gregoria and me got inside the booth for we calypso show and we locked the door behind us, I explained to her everything about this red wire and the microphone and everything else. I told her there was something very funny going on. How I was beginning to suspect all this broadcasting business wasn't nothing more than a big fake, and we were the two firstclass fools to fall for it! Of course, the first thing Gregoria wanted to know logical enough was in that case, what the fuck were Jack and the King doing every night with all those *other* big machines outside blinking away, while we were the two stoolpigeons locked up here inside this booth, singing we hearts out to nobody but those soldiers downstairs inside the parlour? *That*, I told Gregoria, was just what we were about to discover!

And Johnny, scarcely had I finished saying this when I felt the first *good* one begin to come! So I jumped up to throw open the door and hurry outside, and I tapped Jack on he shoulder. Of course, Jack near jumped from out he skin! He turned around to remove the headphones he had clamping around he ears – and this was the first time I noticed the little *microphone* attached to those headphones to *talk* through too – and now Jack wanted to know what the fuck could I *possibly* be doing outside the booth in the middle of my calypso show! I told him it was only for a quick second. Because locked up tight like that inside the little soundproof booth I was afraid to *asphyxiate* poor Gregoria – not to mention my own selfsame-*self* – so please to excuse me for just a moment. Now I turned around to bend over quick and touch my nose to the flooring, my bamsee pointing up straight at he face:

Phuffft-putuffft-thuffft-thuffft-phuffft!

And I took off running back inside the booth to slam the door. Only a minute later Gregoria gave me a smile, and she hurried outside to give the *King* a tap on *he* shoulder this time:

Fooft-pootoofft-tooffft-tooffft-fooft!

Johnny, scarcely had we given them each a couple more of we homestyle BBQ Baked Bean farts, when we heard them drop *broops!* and then *broops!* again, one behind the next flat to the flooring. Because *they* were the ones asphyxiated now out cold unconscious! So all Gregoria and me had to do was to take the precaution of a couple clothespins pinching we noses, and we dragged *them* both inside the DJ booth and shut the door. Of course, we opened it up again to step inside for a few seconds every so often, and we took turns squatting down over they faces to give them another blast. Now, of course, we could put on those headphones straight away, and we could find out whatever it was those two were listening to so intent every night.

Johnny, we couldn't hear nothing a-tall. Nothing more than the same constant *shhh shhh shhh* like air rushing out a punctured tyre. And truth is that after a time we became so *bored* with weselves sitting there we would have nodded off snoring too, if it wasn't for we obligations every couple minutes inside the booth. Then all in a sudden Gregoria gave me a shake, and she told me she heard something in she headphones! So she handed them over and straight away I recognized the voice of my good friend the Sergeant Warren from the Base. He said, 'I just et me a Texas silver sirloin with a heap of mashed per-

194

taters, all smothered in gravy. Woulda reminded you a home, Ike!' And then a moment later whoever was this 'Ike' answered, 'Well you know these dang Brits? Worst egg-flippers in the West! Tell me it's fish 'n chips *again* tonight. Know how they eat 'em? With *vinegar!* And me with my dang seasickness for the big doosie tomorrow. I tell you, I'll be bowing my cookies the whole away across the Channel!'

Of course, it didn't take me *two* seconds to realize who was this famous military personality the Sergeant Warren was conversing with so casual, and of course, I couldn't *never* hold myself back now from butting in my own two-cents neither! I said, 'No, Mr Eisenhower! Don't eat no fried foods if you're going boating tomorrow! Best thing is steamed vegetables, maybe a little light pasta. But Mr Eisenhower, for going to sea fried food is the *worst* possible thing. And don't talk about no *vinegar!*' Of course, before I could even finish talking the line went dead again, and all I heard was the same *shhh shhh shhh*.

So I was thinking this was all very peculiar, but I shrugged my shoulders and gave the headphones back to Gregoria, and put back on my own set again. And it wasn't five minutes before *I* started to hear talking on *my* headphones this time. Only thing was, I can't understand what the man was saying a-tall. Only a set of *sprekem-sprak-spreechem* like if he was spitting on the sidewalk, that soon enough I got vex and I bawled out, 'I don't know what the fuck is all that *sprechem-sprak* you're talking about, but if you want to have a conversation with *me* decent and civilized, you had better learn to speak proper *English!*' Of course, the line went dead again, but then a moment later I heard the person say, 'Please to confirm zein Zee Day tomorrow, sezen June, Normandy Beach between Orne River unt zein St Marcouf, over.'

Of course, I couldn't understand he English no better. But now at least I realized that *other* language he was spitting at me was *German*. And Johnny, I wasn't liking this thing a-tall! On top of that I was beginning to figure out what this Jack and the King were up to with all they fancy radio receivers, and I started to connect things together with Mr Eisenhower going on he boating expedition first thing tomorrow morning. Johnny, before I even had a chance to consider it much, or even plan my strategy, I bawled out to this German whoever he was on the radio: 'No, no, no! *Thursday* moving is Zee Day, whatever the fuck it is you're talking about! Not tomorrow, understand? Zee Day is on Thursday. *Thursday*, you hear? Over?'

Then I heard the German again: 'Confirm. Zee Day is on Zursday. *Zursday*, and *zanks!* Over.'

Now I felt somebody tap *me* on *my* shoulder. And Johnny, now *I* almost jumped from out my skin. And when I turned around I almost dropped in a dead faint flat to the flooring, because who should I find standing there pointing he revolver at me, but my good old friend the Sergeant Warren. The *same* Sergeant Warren I'd just finished having my conversation with happy and friendly enough, only ten minutes before on the same radio! Not only that, but standing there beside him was we own Tanzanian Devil, and he had *he* revolver pointing straight at the head of Gregoria la Rosa!

Of course, Gregoria and me didn't have a clue what was going on – only that those revolvers were real enough, and we didn't want to take no chances – so we took off the headphones clamping around we ears, and raised we hands slow in the air. Now it was that Tanzanian Devil who informed us that he was very sorry to be the one to spill the truth. But all these years we had known him by only he undercover *namenick*. Because he *real* name was Secret Agent Tyrone Davis – and he was not from Australia a-tall with that fakey-fake accent he put on to fool us, but Oklahoma City, Oklahoma – and how he had been waiting all this time only to catch Jack and the King red-handed. Because even though we probably didn't have the slightest suspicion, in fact they were both international spies in cahoots with the Germans! 'The thing is,' Tanzania said now all teary-eyed, all distressed – talking more to *heself* than to either of us or the Sergeant Warren – 'The thing is, *I* never had even the slightest suspicion that my own *betrothed* Gregoria la Rosa, and good old Skip who was almost my own *mother-in-law* too, were both in cahoots with *them!*'

Well! once again I could never hold myself back. I told this Tanzania or Tyrone or who ever the fuck he was that first of all, nobody was *betrothed* to my beloved Gregoria la Rosa unless he performed he duty as a gentleman and begged *my* permission first! And second, didn't he realize that if Gregoria and me were in cahoots with *any*body a-tall, it could *only* be we own Uncle Sam and the US of A. That in fact we had just finished *intercepting* that message Jack and the King were trying to pass to those Germans, and we gave them back a *next* message that will surely have they heads confuffled at least until *Zursday!* Now I turned to Gregoria, and I asked her please to tell me if this thing Tyrone or Tanzania or whoever he was was saying was true? Of course, Gregoria only smiled at me from ear-to-ear all teary-eyed now *sheself* – she held up she left hand to show me the big diamond glittering away on she finger – and even though those two still had they pistols aimed at both we heads, we ignored them just the same, and threw we arms around eachother and let loose a cry of joy!

But now the Sergeant Warren tapped me on my shoulder again. He said he was sorry to be the one to halt we hoopla. 'But Skip,' he said, 'could you please inform us what connection you have to these two extremely dangerous international spies?' Of course, I was so excited with this news of Gregoria, it took me a second to realize that the Sergeant was only talking about we own Jack and the King. I said he would find them both out cold unconscious on the floor of the DJ booth. 'But before you open up that door to wake them up from they sweet dreams,' I told him, 'you might want to take a little *anti-bam-seebomb* precaution first!' And with that I reached to my nose to hand him over the clothespin.

So Johnny, that was that and it marked the end of me and Gregoria's short-lived careers as the world's first female calypsonians, not to mention we *Dee*-Jay fame too. But that was only a small price to pay for the complete success of *Zee*-Day – which, just as you have already discerned – was only the *mis*pronunciation of that German soldier for *Dee*-Day. And that, of course, was the same famous military operation now known to all the world and the history books as the beginning of the end of World War II. Because this same *Dee*-Day – thanks to the help of a little bub-ball from Gregoria and me – General Eisenhower managed to pull off without a hitch. And he caught those Germans by complete surprise with they pantaloons down around they ankles, because they weren't expecting him at least before *Zursday*. And even though the General *did* suffer he typical sea sickness, blowing he cookies the whole way across the English Channel, he also managed to land heself and all he Allied troops on that beach in Normandy safe enough. He managed to break through the defence of those Germans, and in no time a-tall he liberated the city of Paris, then Brussels, and before the month could finish we got the news flash of an attempt to murder Hitler by he own generals. Next thing we heard he'd committed suicide heself, and they shot Mussolini, and Italy surrendered and Germany and then Japan – one after the next like a line of dominoes – and before we could catch we breaths instead of fighting-down and killing-up each other, the whole world was playing Carnival in the streets!

Of course, it was we happy ending too. Because now at last we have reached the part of Gregoria la Rosa's marriage to the boy from Oklahoma, we very own Tanzanian Devil. Because I told him that after all these years, I could never learn to call him *Tyrone Davis,* no more than he could learn to call me nothing more than *Skip.* Johnny, I gave them the *biggest* pappyshow wedding Corpus Christi has ever seen. With Sergeant Warren as the handsome best man in he white uniform with all the gold stripes, and braids, and epaulets, and me of course as the beautiful bridesmaid, with my hat so big I had to turn to the side only to be able to pass through the door! We held the reception right here in the house. And Johnny, let me tell you *that* was a fête too! Gregoria and me filled the whole yard with tables and chairs and bouquets of white roses. We cooked for two weeks in advance, and we had the champagne flowing, with those boys all saying the *only* good reason for fighting a war like that, was to finish with a party like this!

Of course, when dinner was over we had plenty big speeches. Sergeant Warren rose to the podium to give us he toast to the bride, and he compared her to a sea nymph from out the sonnets of Shakespeare! It was he duty also to thank the mother of the bride. A woman, he said, known to every smiling boy here as we own beloved Skip, and I hereby pronounce her the

Official Adopted Mother of all the American Troops!

So everybody clapped they hands together, and when the Sergeant sat down Tanzania rose to the podium. It was he duty to toast the bridesmaid – who of course was *me* too – but he only apologized and said how he'd never been a man of many fancy words. On the other hand, he said, he happened to know a very beautiful and gracious young widow who *was.* 'So Skip,' he told me, 'as the only appropriate finale for a great fête like this, would you please give us the pleasure of recounting for us one of you famous tales!' Of course, next thing you know they were all clapping they hands together, whistling on they fingers and beating they forks against they champagne glasses. So even though I was exhausted to my bones after all this commess, I didn't have *no* choice but to rise to the podium myself.

I gave a few taps on that fancy Saturn-shaped microphone to make sure it was working loud and clear, and I told them please to forgive me if the champagne had gone a little bit to my head. Forgive me if it had made me a little bit more sentimental than usual. But even though this was a very *joyous* occasion for me, it was a very sad occasion also. Because not only was I about to lose my own beloved daughter Gregoria la Rosa – who would soon be living in this place called *Oklahoma* that I couldn't even pronounce it proper, less still to try to find it on the big map – but I would also be losing my young American soldiers, who had all become like my own sons to me. 'Because soon enough,' I told them, 'you will be folding up you big Base like a pack of cards, and you will be sending it back home to America too.'

'Boys, Sergeant Warren – and *especially* my new friend the General Eisenhower – who as you all know happened to be visiting we small island on he way back to the States, and who has paid us the great honour of being with us here this afternoon. *All* my cherished guests. And I would be remiss in truth if I failed to mention we guest of honour tonight, we own Captain On-the-eggs!, sitting there at the head table with General Eisenhower too – and between them my *other* beloved daughter, Indra – beautiful as ever in she elegant red velvet gown. That I can only hope the good General won't be *permanently* cross-eyed by the end of tonight, since he hasn't raised he nose for an instant from Indra's tantalizing tot-tots – ready to burst at any moment from she exquisite dress! – but perhaps *that* pleasant expectation will entice the General to visit these shores one day again.'

Now I moved the microphone a little closer, and I repeated myself, 'All my cherished friends and guests: let me say that we hope you have enjoyed we hospitality. Let me be the first to offer you a very pleasant *bon voyage*, and say that we wish that you could have remained with us awhile longer. But now it is time for *us* to make we *own* return trip home, whether we are prepared for this voyage or not. And even though *we* voyage is the shortest distance, even though we own is the quickest, it is the longest and most difficult journey of all. But this,' I told them, 'is no kind of occasion to dwell on the uncertain future. So let we instead try to remember some of those sad, happy times that we have shared together in these sad, happy times of the war. For me, there is only *one* way!'

Johnny, now I went on to relate them a short one.